I0682952

THE FIRE PEOPLE

Start Publishing PD LLC
Copyright © 2024 by Start Publishing PD LLC

All rights reserved, including the right to reproduce this book or portions thereof in any form whatsoever.

Start Publishing PD is a registered trademark of Start Publishing PD LLC
Manufactured in the United States of America

Cover art: Shutterstock/Taisiya Kozorez

Cover design: Jennifer Do

10 9 8 7 6 5 4 3 2 1

ISBN 979-8-8809-1563-7

THE FIRE PEOPLE

by Ray Cummings

THE COMING OF THE LIGHT

The first of the new meteors landed on the earth in November, 1940. It was discovered by a farmer in his field near Brookline, Massachusetts, shortly after daybreak on the morning of the 11th. Astronomically, the event was recorded by the observatory at Harvard as the sudden appearance of what apparently was a new star, increasing in the short space of a few hours from invisibility to a power beyond that of the first magnitude, and then as rapidly fading again to invisibility. This star was recorded by two of the other great North American observatories, and by one in the Argentine Republic. That it was comparatively small in mass and exceedingly close to the earth, even when first discovered, was obvious. All observers agreed that it was a heavenly body of an entirely new order.

The observatory at Harvard supplemented its account by recording the falling, just before dawn of the 11th, of an extraordinarily brilliant meteor that flamed with a curious red and green light as it entered the earth's atmosphere. This meteor did not burn itself out, but fell, still retaining its luminosity, from a point near the zenith, to the horizon.

What the farmer saw was a huge fire burning near the center of his field. It was circular in form and about thirty feet in diameter. He was astonished to see it there, but what surprised him more was its peculiar aspect.

It was still the twilight of dawn when he reached the field. He beheld the fire first from a point several hundred yards away. As he explained it, the light—for it was more aptly described as a light than a fire—extended in parallel rays from the ground directly upward into the sky. He could see no line of demarkation where it ended at the top. It seemed to extend into the sky an infinite distance. It was, in fact, as though an enormous search -light were buried in his field, casting its beam of light directly upward.

But more than all this, the farmer was struck by the extraordinary color of the light. At the base it was a deep, solid green. This green color extended upward for perhaps fifty feet, then it shaded into red. The farmer noticed, too, that the fire did not leap and dance with flames, but seemed rather to glow—a steady light like the burning of colored powder. In the morning half -light it threw a weird, unearthly reddish -green glow over the field.

The farmer approached to within twenty feet of the light. He looked to see what was burning, but could not determine, for the greenish base extended directly down into the ground. He noticed also that it gave out extraordinarily little heat. The morning was not exceptionally cold, yet he stood within twenty feet of the fire without discomfort.

I was on the staff of the Boston Observer at this time. I reached Brookline about noon of the 11th of November, and went directly to the field where the fire was burning. Nearly a thousand people were there, watching.

By daylight the fire still held its green and red color, although its light was much less intense. It held its characteristic shape. Though clearly definable, under the rays of the sun it became quite transparent. Looking through it, I could see plainly the crowd of people on the farther side of the field. The effect was similar to looking through a faintly tinted glass, except that now I noticed that the light had a sort of crawling motion, like the particles of a heavy fog. The fire came from a hole in the ground; by daylight now the hole could be seen plainly.

For some moments I stood silent, awestruck by this extraordinary spectacle. Then a man standing beside me remarked that there was no smoke. I had not thought of that before, but it was true—indeed, the fire appeared phosphorescent.

"Let's get up closer," said the man beside me.

Together we walked to within ten feet of the outer edge of the fire. We could feel its heat now, although it was not uncomfortable except when it beat directly on our faces. Standing so close, we could see down into the hole from which the light emanated.

Lying at the bottom of the hole, perhaps ten feet below the surface, I saw the jagged top of an enormous gray sphere, burned and pitted. This was the meteor—nearly thirty feet in diameter—that in its fall had buried itself deep in the loam of the field.

As we stood there looking down into the hole some one across from us tossed in a ball of paper. It seemed to hang poised a moment, then it shriveled up, turned black, and floated slowly down until it rested on top of the sphere.

Some one else threw a block of wood about a foot long into the hole. I could see it as it struck the top of the sphere. It lay there an instant; then it, too, turned black and charred, but it did not burst into flame.

The man beside me plucked at my sleeve. "Why don't it burn?" he asked.

I shook myself loose.

"How should I know?" I answered impatiently.

I found myself trembling all over with an unreasoning fear, for there was something uncanny about the whole affair. I went back to Brookline soon after that to send in the story and do some telephoning. When I got back to the field I saw a man in front of me carrying a pail of water. I fell into step beside him.

"What do you suppose it'll do?" he asked as we walked along.

"God knows," I answered. "Try it."

But when we got down into the field we found the police authorities in charge. The crowd was held back now in a circle, a hundred yards away from the light. After some argument we got past the officials, and, followed by two camera men and a motion -picture man who bobbed up from nowhere, walked out across the cleared space toward the light. We stopped about six or eight feet from the edge of the hole; the heat was uncomfortably intense.

"I'll make a dash for it," said the man with the pail.

He ran forward a few steps, splashed the water into the light, and hastily retreated. As the water struck the edge of the light there came a roar like steam escaping under tremendous pressure; a great cloud of vapor rolled back over us and dissolved. When the air cleared I saw that the light, or the fire of this mysterious agency, was unchanged. The water dashed against it had had absolutely no effect.

It was just after this incident that the first real tragedy happened. One of the many quadruplanes that had been circling over the field during the afternoon passed directly over the light at an altitude of perhaps three thousand feet. We saw it sail away erratically, as though its pilot no longer had it under control. Then it suddenly burst into flame and came quivering down in a long, lengthening spiral of smoke.

That night the second of the meteors landed on the earth. It fell near Juneau, Alaska, and was accompanied by the same phenomena as the one we were watching. The reports showed it to be slightly smaller in size than the Brookline meteor. It burned brightly during the day of November 12. On the morning of the 13th wireless reports from Alaska stated that it had burned out during the previous night.

Meanwhile the light at Brookline was under constant surveillance. It remained unchanged in all respects.

The next night it rained—a heavy, pelting downpour. For a mile or more around the field the hissing of steam could be heard as the rain struck the light. The next morning was clear, and still we saw no change in the light.

THE FIRE PEOPLE

Then, a week later, came the cold spell of 1940. Surpassing in severity the winters of 1888 and 1918, it broke all existing records of the Weather Bureau. The temperature during the night of November 20, at Brookline, fell to thirty degrees below zero. During this night the fire was seen to dwindle gradually in size, and by morning it was entirely extinguished.

No other meteors fell that winter; and, as their significance remained unexplained, public interest in them soon died out. The observatories at Harvard, Flagstaff, Cordoba, and the newer one on Table Mountain, near Cape Town, all reported the appearance of several new stars, flaring into prominence for a few hours and visible just after sunset and before dawn, on several nights during November. But these published statements were casually received and aroused only slight general comment.

Then, in February, 1941, came the publication of Professor Newland's famous theory of the Mercutian Light—as the fire was afterward known. Professor Newland was at this time the foremost astronomer in America, and his extraordinary theory and the predictions he made, coming from so authoritative a source, amazed and startled the world.

His paper, couched in the language of science, was rewritten to the public understanding and published in the newspapers of nearly every country. It was an exhaustive scientific deduction, explaining in theory the origin of the two meteors that had fallen to earth two months before.

In effect Professor Newland declared that the curious astronomical phenomena of the previous November—the new "stars" observed, the two meteors that had fallen with their red and green light -fire—were all evidence of the existence of intelligent life on the planet Mercury.

I give you here only the more important parts of the paper as it was rewritten for the public prints:

... I am therefore strongly inclined to accept the theory advanced by Schiaparelli in 1882, in which he concluded that Mercury rotates on its axis once in eighty -eight days. Now, since the sidereal revolution of Mercury, i.e., its complete revolution around the sun, occupies only slightly under eighty -eight days, the planet always presents the same face to the sun. On that side reigns perpetual day; on the other—the side presented to the earth as Mercury passes us—perpetual night.

The existence of an atmospheric envelope on Mercury, to temper the extremes of heat and cold that would otherwise exist on its light and dark hemispheres, seems fairly certain. If there were no atmosphere on the planet, temperatures on that face toward the sun would be extraordinarily high—many hundred degrees hotter than the boiling point of water.

Quite the other extreme would be the conditions on the dark side, for without the sheltering blanket of an atmosphere, this surface must be exposed to the intense cold of interplanetary space.

I have reason to believe, however, particularly from my deductions made in connection with the photographs taken during the transit of Mercury over the face of the sun on November 11 last, that there does exist an atmosphere on this planet—an atmosphere that appears to be denser and more cloudy than our own. I am led to this conclusion by other evidence that has long been fairly generally accepted as fact. The terminating edge of the phases of Mercury is not sharp, but diffuse and shaded—there is here an atmospheric penumbra. The spectroscope also shows lines of absorption, which proves that Mercury has a gaseous envelope thicker than ours.

This atmosphere, whatever may be its nature I do not assume, tempers the heat and cold on Mercury to a degree comparable to the earth. But I do believe that it makes the planet—on its dark face particularly—capable of supporting intelligent life of some form.

Mercury was in transit over the face of the sun on November 11, of last year, within a few hours of the time the first meteor fell to earth. The planet was therefore at one of her closest points to the earth, and—this is significant—was presenting her dark face toward us.

At this time several new "stars" were reported, flashing into brilliancy and then fading again into obscurity. All were observed in the vicinity of Mercury; none appeared elsewhere. I believe these so -called "stars" to be some form of interplanetary vehicle—probably navigated in space by beings from Mercury. And from them were launched the two meteors that struck our planet. How many others were dispatched that may have missed their mark we have no means of determining.

The days around November 11 last, owing to the proximity of Mercury to the earth, were most favorable for such a bombardment. A similar time is now once more almost upon us!

Because of the difference in the velocities of Mercury and the earth in their revolutions around the sun, one synodic revolution of Mercury, i.e., from one inferior conjunction to the next, requires nearly one hundred and sixteen days. In eighty-eight days Mercury has completed her sidereal revolution, but during that time the earth has moved ahead a distance requiring twenty-eight days more before she can be overtaken.

After the first week in March of this year therefore Mercury will again be approaching inferior conjunction, and again will pass at her closest point to the earth.

We may expect at this time another bombardment of a severity that may cause tremendous destruction, or destroy entirely life on this planet!

THE UNKNOWN ENEMY

When, in February, 1941, Professor James Newland issued this remarkable statement, my paper sent me at once to interview him. He was at this time at the head of the Harvard observatory staff. He lived with his son and daughter in Cambridge. His wife was dead. I had been acquainted with the professor and his family for some time. I first met his son, Alan, during our university days at Harvard. We liked each other at once, and became firm friends—possibly because we were such opposite physical types, as sometimes happens.

Alan was tall, lean and muscular—an inch or so over six feet—with the perfect build of an athlete. I am dark; Alan was blond, with short, curly hair, and blue eyes. His features were strong and regular. He was, in fact, one of the handsomest men I have ever seen. And yet he acted as though he didn't know it—or if he did, as though he considered it a handicap. I think what saved him was his ingenious, ready smile, and his retiring, unassuming—almost diffident—manner.

At the time of the events I am describing Alan was twenty-two—about two years younger than I. It was his first year out of college. He had taken a scientific course and intended to join his father's staff.

Beth and Alan were twins. I was tremendously interested in Beth even then. She seemed one of the most worth-while girls I had ever met. She was a little wisp of femininity, slender and delicate, hardly more than five feet one or two. She had beautiful golden hair and an animated, pretty face, with a pert little snub nose. She was a graduate of Vassar, and planned to take up chemistry as a profession, for she had the same scientific bent as her father and brother.

I called upon Professor Newland the evening of the day his statement was published, and found all three discussing it.

"You want me to talk for publication, don't you, Bob Trevor?" the professor asked suddenly, after we had exchanged a few pleasantries.

He was a wiry little man, about sixty, smooth-shaven, with sparse gray hair, a rugged face of strong character, and a restless air of energy about him. He was an indefatigable worker; indeed, I am confident that, for any single continuous period of work without sleep, he could have run Alan and me into the ground and still have been comparatively fresh.

"You want an exclusive follow-up story from me to-night, don't you?" he repeated.

11

I admitted that I did.

"What you'll get won't be just what you expect. Look at this."

He pulled one of the evening papers toward him vigorously. "They think it is humorous. There—read that."

The item to which he pointed was a sprightly account of the weird beings that might shortly arrive from Mercury.

"They think it's a joke—some of them. There's another—read that."

The attitude of the press was distinctly an inclination to treat the affair from the humorous side. I had seen indications of that during the day at the office.

"Look here, Bob"—the professor swept all the papers aside with his hand. "You put it to them this way. Make them see this is not a prediction of the end of the world. We've had those before—nobody pays any attention to them, and rightly so. But this Mercutian Light is more than a theory—it's a fact. We fought it last November, and we'll have to fight it again next month. That's what I want to make them realize."

"They'll think it is worth being serious about," Alan put in, "if one of those lights drop into Boston or New York—especially if it happens to play in a horizontal direction instead of vertical."

We went into the whole subject thoroughly, and the professor gave me a second signed statement in which he called upon the nations of the world to prepare for the coming peril.

The actual characteristics of the Mercutian Light we had discussed before several times. A good deal had been printed about it during the previous December—without, as I have said, attracting much public attention. The two meteors had been examined. They were found to be of a mineral that could have originated on Mercury. They were burned and pitted like other meteorites by their passage through the earth's atmosphere.

Of the light itself Professor Newland had already given his opinion. It was, he said, some unknown form of etheric vibration. It radiated heat very slightly, but it had the peculiarity of generating intense heat in anything it touched directly.

"You'd better explain that, father," said Beth, when we reached this point in our summary that evening.

"Heat is the vibration of molecules of matter," the professor began.

I nodded.

"Make it clear when you write it up, Bob," Alan put in. "It's like this. All molecules are in motion—the faster the motion, the hotter the substance, and vice versa."

"And this Mercutian Light," Beth added, "has the power of enormously increasing the molecular vibration of anything it comes in contact with—"

"But it doesn't radiate much heat itself," Alan finished.

Professor Newland smiled. "The old man doesn't have much of a show, does he?"

Alan sat down somewhat abashed, but Beth remained standing beside her father, listening intently to everything he said.

"This light I conceive to be the chief weapon of warfare of the Mercutians," the professor went on. "There has been some talk of those two meteors being signals. That's all nonsense. They were not signals—they were missiles. It was an act of aggression."

I tried to get him to give some idea of what the inhabitants of Mercury might be like, for that was what my editor chiefly desired.

At first he would say nothing along those lines.

"That is pure speculation," he explained. "And very easy speculation, too. Any one can allow his imagination to run wild and picture strange beings of another world. I don't predict they will actually land on the earth—and I have no idea what they will look like if they do land. As a matter of fact, they will probably look very much like ourselves. I see no reason to doubt it."

"Like us?" I ejaculated.

"Why not?" said Alan. "Conditions on Mercury are not fundamentally different from here. We don't have to conceive any very extraordinary sort of being to fill them."

"Here's what you can tell your paper," said the professor abruptly. "Take it down."

I took out my notebook, and he dictated briskly.

"Regarding the possible characteristics of inhabitants of Mercury, it is my conception that intelligent life—let us say, human life—wherever it exists in our universe does not greatly differ in character from that of our own planet. Mars, Venus, Mercury, even Neptune, are relatively close. I believe the Creator has constructed all human life on the same general plan.

"I believe that, being neighbors—if I may be permitted the expression—it is intended that intercourse between the planets should take place. That we have been isolated up to the present time is only because of our ignorance—our inability to bridge the gap. I believe that migration, friendship, commerce, even war, between the inhabitants of different planets of our solar system was intended by Almighty God—and, in good time, will come to pass.

"This is not science; and yet science does not contradict it, in my opinion. Human life on Mercury, Venus or Mars may need bodies taller, shorter, heavier, lighter, more fragile or more solid than ours. The organs will differ from ours, perhaps, but not materially so. The senses will be the same.

"In a word, I believe that nearly all the range of diversity of human life existing on any of the planets exists now on this earth, or has existed in the past, or will exist in the future through our own development, or at most the differences would not be greater than a descent into our animal kingdom would give us.

"Mercutians may have the sense of smell developed to the point of a dog; the instinct of direction of the homing pigeon; the eyes of a cat in the dark, or an owl in the light; but I cannot conceive of them being so different that similar illustrations would not apply.

"I believe the Creator intends intercourse of some kind, friendly or unfriendly, to take place between the worlds. As China was for centuries, so for eons we of this earth have been isolated. That time is past. The first act was one of aggression. Let us wait for the next calmly but soberly, with full realization of the danger. For we may be—indeed, I think we are—approaching the time of greatest peril that human life on this earth has ever had to face!"

THE LANDING OF THE INVADERS

March 8, 1941, was the date at which Mercury was again to be in inferior conjunction—at her closest point to the earth since her transit over the face of the sun on November 11 of the previous year. During February—after Professor Newland's statements—the subject received a tremendous amount of publicity. Some scientific men rallied to Professor Newland's support; others scouted the idea as absurd.

Officially, the governments of the world ignored the matter entirely. In general, the press, editorially, wrote in a humorous vein, conjuring up many ridiculous possibilities of what was about to happen. The public followed this lead. It was amused, interested to a degree; but, as a mass, neither apprehensive nor serious—only curious.

In some parts of the earth—among the smaller Latin nations particularly—some apprehension was felt. But even so, no one knew what to do about it—where to go to avoid the danger—for the attack, if it came at all, was as likely to strike one country as another.

The first week in March arrived with public interest steadily increasing. Mercury, always difficult of observation, presented no spectacle for the public gaze and imagination to feed upon. But, all over the world, there were probably more eyes turned toward the setting and rising sun during that week than ever had been turned there before.

Professor Newland issued no more statements after that evening I have described. He was taken with a severe cold in the latter part of February, and as Beth was in delicate health and did not stand the Northern winters well, the whole family left for a few months' stay at their bungalow home in Florida. They were quite close to the little village of Bay Head, on the Gulf coast. I kept in communication with them there.

The 8th of March came and passed without a report from any part of the earth of the falling of the Mercutian meteors. Satirical comment in the press doubled. There was, indeed, no scientific report of any unusual astronomical phenomena, except from the Harvard observatory the following morning. There Professor Newland's assistant, Professor Brighton, stated he had again observed a new "star"—an interplanetary vehicle, as Professor Newland described it. Only a single one had been observed this time. It was seen just before dawn of the 9th.

15

THE FIRE PEOPLE

Then, about 4 P.M., Atlantic time, on the afternoon of the 9th, the world was electrified by the report of the landing of invaders in the United States. The news came by wireless from Billings, Montana. An interplanetary vehicle of huge size had landed on the desert in the Shoshone River district of northern Wyoming, west of the Big Horn Mountains.

This strange visitor—it was described as a gleaming, silvery object perhaps a hundred feet in diameter—had landed near the little Mormon settlement of Byron. The hope that its mission might be friendly was dispelled even in the first report from Billings. The characteristic red and green light-fire had swept the country near by—a horizontal beam this time—and the town of Byron was reported destroyed, and in all likelihood with the loss of its entire population.

The Boston Observer sent me to Billings almost immediately by quadruplane. I arrived there about eight o'clock on the evening of the 10th. The city was in a turmoil. Ranchers from the neighboring cattle country thronged its streets. A perfect exodus of people—Mormons and oil men from Shoshone country, almost the entire populations of Cody, Powell, Garland, and other towns near the threatened section, the Indians from the Crow Reservation at Frannie—all were streaming through Billings.

The Wyoming State Airplane Patrol, gathered in a squadron by orders from Cheyenne, occasionally passed overhead, flashing huge white searchlights. I went immediately to the office of the Billings Dispatch. It was so crowded I could not get in. From what I could pick up among the excited, frightened people of Billings, and the various bulletins that the Dispatch had sent out during the day, the developments of the first twenty-four hours of Mercutian invasion were these:

Only a single "vehicle"—we called it that for want of a better name—had landed. Airplane observation placed its exact position on the west bank of the Shoshone River, about four miles southwest of Byron and the same distance southeast of Garland. The country here is typically that of the Wyoming desert—sand and sagebrush—slightly rolling in some places, with occasional hills and buttes.

The Chicago, Burlington and Quincy Railroad runs down its spur from the Northern Pacific near Billings, passes through the towns of Frannie—near the border of Montana and Wyoming—and Garland, and terminates at Cody. This line, running special trains throughout the day, had brought up a large number of people. During the afternoon a bomb of some kind—it was vaguely described as a variation of the red and green light -rays—had destroyed one of the trains near Garland. The road was now open only down to Frannie.

The town of Byron, I learned, was completely annihilated. It had been swept by the Mercutian Light and destroyed by fire. Garland was as yet unharmed. There was broken country between it and the Mercutian invaders, and the rays of the single light which they were using could not reach it directly.

Such, briefly, was the situation as I found it that evening of the 10th. In Billings we were sixty -five miles north of the Mercutian landing place. What power for attack and destruction the enemy had, we had no means of determining. How many of them there were; how they could travel over the country; what the effective radius of their light -fire was; the nature of the "bomb" that had destroyed the train on the C., B. and Q. near the town of Garland—all those were questions that no one could answer.

Billings was, during those next few days, principally a gathering place and point of departure for refugees. Yet, so curiously is the human mind constituted, underneath all this turmoil the affairs of Billings went on as before. The stores did not close; the Billings Dispatch sent out its reports; the Northern Pacific trains from east and west daily brought their quota of reporters, picture men and curiosity seekers, and took away all who had sense enough to go. The C., B. and Q. continued running trains to Frannie—which was about fifteen miles from the Mercutian landing place—and many of the newspaper men, most of those, in fact, who did not have airplanes, went there.

That first evening in Billings, Rolland Mercer—a chap about my own age, who had brought me from the East in one of the Boston Observer's planes—and I, decided on a short flight about the neighboring country to look the situation over. We started about midnight, a crisp, cloudless night with no moon. We had been warned against venturing into the danger zone; several of the Wyoming patrol and numbers of private planes had been seen to fall in flames when the light struck them.

We had no idea what the danger zone was—how close we dared go—but decided to chance it. To fly sufficiently high for safety directly over the Mercutians appeared difficult, since the light -fire already had proven effective at a distance of several miles at least. We decided not to attempt that, but merely to follow the course of the C., B. and Q. southwest to Cody, then to circle around to the east, and thence back north to Billings, passing well to the east of the Mercutians.

THE FIRE PEOPLE

We started, as I have said, about midnight, rising from the rolling prairie back of Billings. We climbed five hundred feet and, with our searchlight playing upon the ground beneath, started directly for Frannie. We passed over Frannie at about eight hundred feet, and continued on the C., B. and Q. line toward Garland. We had decided to pass to a considerable extent to the west of Garland, to be farther away from the danger, and then to strike down to Cody.

We were flying now at a speed close to a hundred and forty miles an hour. Off to the left I could see the red and green beam of the single light of the Mercutians; it was pointing vertically up into the air, motionless. Something—I do not know what—made me decide to turn off our searchlight.

I looked behind us. Some miles away, and considerably nearer the Mercutians than we were, I saw the light of another plane. I was watching it when suddenly the red and green beam swung toward it, and a moment later picked it up. I caught a fleeting glimpse of what I took to be a little biplane. It remained for an instant illuminated by the weird red and green flare; then the Mercutian Light swung back to its vertical position. A second later the biplane burst into flames and fell.

The thing left me shuddering. I turned our searchlight permanently off and sat staring down at the shadowy country scurrying away beneath us.

Mercer had evidently not seen this tragedy. He did not look at me, but kept facing the front. We were now somewhat to the west of Garland, with it between us and the Mercutians. The few lights of the town could be seen plainly. The country beneath us seemed fairly level. To the west, half a mile away, perhaps, I could make out a sheer, perpendicular wall of rock. We seemed to be flying parallel with it and about level with its top.

We were rising a little, I think, when suddenly our engines stopped. I remember it flashed through my mind to wonder how Mercer would dare shut them off when we were flying so low. The sudden silence confused me a little. I started to ask him if he had seen the biplane fall, when he swung back abruptly and gripped me by the arm.

"Turn on the light—you fool—we've got to land!"

I fumbled with the searchlight. Then, just as I turned the switch, I saw, rising from a point near the base of the Mercutian Light, what appeared to be a skyrocket.

It rose in a long, graceful arc, reached the top of its ascent, and came down, still flaming. I remember deciding it would fall in or near Garland.

It seemed to go out just before it landed—at least I did not follow it all the way down. Then there came a flash as though a huge quantity of red and green smokeless powder had gone off in a puff; a brief instant of darkness, and then flames rose from a hundred points in the little town. The next second our wheels ground in the sand.

I heard a splintering crash; something struck me violently on the shoulder; then—blackness.

THE MEETING

Professor Newland and his family were living in seclusion in their Florida home at the time the Mercutian invaders landed in Wyoming. The curious events in Florida, which connected them so directly with the invasion and caused Alan later to play so vital a part in it, are so important that I am impelled to relate them chronologically, rather than as they were told me afterward by Alan and Beth.

When, on March 9, the news that the Mercutians had landed in Wyoming reached Professor Newland, he immediately established telegraphic communication with Harvard. Thus he was kept fully informed on the situation—indeed, he saw it as a whole far better than I did.

On March 12, three days after the landing, orders from Washington were given out, regulating all passenger transportation in the direction of the danger zone. One hundred miles was the limit set. State troops were placed on all trains, State roads were likewise guarded, and the State airplane patrols united in a vigilant effort to keep outside planes from getting in. On the 13th the President of the United States issued an appeal to all persons living within the hundred-mile limit, asking them to leave.

On March 14 the Canadian government offered its assistance in any way possible—its Saskatchewan airplane patrol was already helping Montana maintain the hundred-mile limit. Similar offers were immediately made by nearly every government in the world.

Such were the first main steps taken to safeguard the people.

By March 14 the actual conditions of affairs in the threatened section of Wyoming was fairly well known. The town of Garland was destroyed by fire on the night of the 10th, and the towns of Mantua and Powell—north and south of Garland respectively—the following morning. On the evening of the 11th a government plane, flying without lights, sacrificed itself in an attempt to drop a bomb into the Mercutian camp. It was caught by the light when almost directly over the Mercutians, and was seen to fall in flames.

It was estimated that the single light was controlling an area with a radius of about ten miles. To the south and west there was practically nothing but desert. To the west Garland, Mantua and Powell were burned. To the north Deaver and Crowley—on another branch of the C., B. and Q., about ten miles from the

Mercutians—were as yet unharmed. They were, however, entirely deserted by the 15th.

During these days the Mercutians did not move from their first landing place. Newspaper speculation regarding their capabilities for offensive action ran rife. Perhaps they could not move. They appeared to possess but one ray of light -fire; this had an effective radius of ten miles. The only other offensive weapon shown was the rocket, or bomb, that had destroyed the C., B. and Q. train near Garland and the town itself. Reports differed as to what had set fire to the town of Powell.

All these points were less than ten miles away from the Mercutian base. Obviously, then, the danger was grossly exaggerated. The unknown invaders could safely and easily be shelled by artillery from a much greater distance. Mercury had passed inferior conjunction; no other Mercutian vehicles had been reported as landing anywhere on the earth. A few days, and the danger would be over. Thus the newspapers of the country settled the affair.

On March 14th it was announced that General Price would conduct the military operations against the Mercutians. Press dispatches simultaneously announced that troops, machine guns and artillery were being rushed to Billings. This provoked a caustic comment from the Preparedness League of America, to the effect that no military operations of any offensive value could be conducted by the United States against anybody or anything.

This statement was to some extent true. During the twenty years that had elapsed since the World War armament of all kinds had fallen into disuse. Few improvements in offensive weapons had been made. The military organization and equipment of the United States, and, indeed, that of many of the other great powers, was admittedly inadequate to cope with any very powerful enemy.

Professor Newland telegraphed to the War Department at Washington on the 14th, stating that in his opinion new scientific measures would have to be devised to deal with this enemy, and that whatever scientific knowledge he had on the subject was at their disposal at their request. To this telegram the government never replied.

It was a day or two after that—on the morning of the 16th, to be exact—that the next most important development in this strange affair took place. Alan Newland rose that morning at dawn and took his launch for a trip up one of the neighboring bayous. He was alone, and intended to fish for an hour or so and return home in time for breakfast.

THE FIRE PEOPLE

He went, perhaps, three miles up the winding little stream. Then, just after sunrise, he shut off the motor and drifted silently along. The bayou split into two streams here, coming together again a quarter of a mile farther on, and thus forming a little island. It was just past the point of this island that Alan shut off his motor.

He had been sitting quiet several minutes preparing his tackle, when his eye caught something moving behind the dark green of the magnolia trees hanging over the low banks of the island. It seemed to be a flicker of red and white some five feet above the ground. Instinctively he reached for the little rifle he had brought with him to shoot at it, thinking it might be a bird, although he had never seen one before of such a color.

A moment later, in the silence, he heard a rustling of the palmettos near the bank of the bayou. He waited, quiet, with the rifle across his knees. His launch was still moving forward slowly from the impetus of the motor. And then, quite suddenly, he came into sight of the figure of a girl standing motionless beside a tree on the island a few feet back from the water and evidently watching him.

Alan was startled. He knew there was no one living on the island. There were, in fact, few people at all in the vicinity—only an occasional negro shack or the similar shack of the "poor white trash," and a turpentine camp, several miles back in the pines.

But it was not the presence of the girl here on the island at daybreak that surprised him most, but the appearance of the girl herself. He sat staring at her dumbly, wondering if he were awake or dreaming. For the girl—who otherwise might have appeared nothing more than an extraordinarily beautiful young female of this earth, somewhat fantastically dressed—the girl had wings!

He rubbed his eyes and looked again. There was no doubt about it—they were huge, deep -red feathered wings, reaching from her shoulder blades nearly to the ground. She took a step away from the tree and flapped them once or twice idly. Alan could see they would measure nearly ten feet from tip to tip when outstretched. His launch had lost its forward motion now, and for the moment was lying motionless in the sluggish bayou. Hardly fifty feet separated him from the girl.

Her eyes stared into his for a time—a quiet, curious stare, with no hint of fear in it. Then she smiled. Her lips moved, but the soft words that reached him across the water were in a language he could not understand. But he comprehended her gesture; it distinctly bade him come ashore. Alan took a new grip on himself, gathered his scattered wits, and tried to think connectedly.

He laid his rifle in the bottom of the launch; then, just as he was reaching for an oar, he saw back among the tall cabbage palms on the island in an open space, a glowing, silvery object, like a house painted silver and shining under the rays of a brilliant sun.

Then the whole thing came to him. He remembered the press descriptions from Wyoming of the Mercutian vehicle. He saw this white rectangle on the little Florida island as a miniature of that which had brought the invaders of Wyoming from space. And then this girl—

Fear for an instant supplanted amazement in Alan Newland's heart. He looked around. He could see back into the trees plainly, almost across the island. He stood up in the boat. There seemed no one else in sight.

Alan sat down and, taking up the oar, sculled the launch toward the spot where the girl was standing. His mind still refused to think clearly. The vague thought came to him that he might be struck dead by some unknown power the instant he landed. Then, as he again met the girl's eyes—a clear, direct, honest gaze with something of a compelling dignity in it—his fear suddenly left him.

A moment later the bow of the launch pushed its way through the wire grass and touched the bank. Alan laid aside his oar, tied the boat to a half -submerged log, and stepped ashore.

CAPTURED!

When I recovered consciousness I found myself lying in the sand with Mercer sitting beside me. It was still night. The tangled wreckage of our airplane lay near by; evidently Mercer had carried me out of it.

I sat up.

"I'm all right," I said. "What happened?"

He grinned at me with relief.

"The damned engine stopped. I don't know what was the matter. You had the light off. I couldn't see anything when we got down close."

He waved his hand toward the wrecked plane.

"It's done for," he added; "but I'm not hurt much. Are you?"

"No," I said. "I'm all right."

I climbed to my feet unsteadily; my head seemed about to split open.

"Garland's burning," he added.

Over the desert, some two or three miles away, the burning town could be seen plainly.

"What are we going to do?" Mercer asked after a moment.

I was pretty weak and badly bruised all over. Mercer seemed to have fared better than I. We talked over our situation at length. Finally we decided to rest where we were until daybreak. I would feel better then, and we could start back on foot for Mantua and Frannie.

I lay down again—my head was going round like a top—and Mercer sat beside me. It was pretty cold, but we were warmly dressed and not uncomfortable. The fact that we were so close to the Mercutians—not much over seven or eight miles—worried us a little. But we reasoned that we were in no great danger. We could still see their light -ray standing vertically in the air.

Occasionally it would swing slowly to one side or the other. Once it swung toward us, but as its base was in a hollow, it was cut off by the higher ground between as it swung down, and we knew it could not reach us from that position.

After a while I fell asleep. When Mercer woke me up it was dawn.

"Let's get started," he said. "I'm hungry as the devil."

I felt much better now. I was hungry myself, and stiff, and chilled.

"You'll feel better walking," he added. "Come on. It'll take us a deuce of a while over this sand."

We decided to strike for the railroad at its closest point to us. The State automobile road to Cody ran along near the railroad, and we planned to follow that up to Mantua.

After a last look at our plane, which was hopelessly demolished, we started off, heading north of Garland. We had been walking along a few minutes when Mercer suddenly gripped me by the arm. I followed the direction of his glance. Another rocket was rising from the Mercutian base. It was still dark enough for us to see its flare as it rose and curved in a long, graceful arc. We stopped stock still and stood watching. The rocket arched over to the north. As it came down we lost sight of it.

"That went into Mantua," said Mercer in a horrified whisper.

A moment later we saw, in the direction of Mantua, that brief, silent, smokeless red and green flash. Then the sky lighted up a lurid red, and we knew Mantua was burning.

We stood looking at each other for a time, too frightened and horrified for words. The thing was not like modern warfare. It was uncanny in its silent deadliness, and there seemed a surety about it that was appalling.

"We're cut off," said Mercer finally.

His face was white and his voice trembled.

We were both pretty much unnerved, but after a moment we got ourselves together and talked calmly about what was best for us to do.

We concluded finally to go ahead to the road. We calculated we were not over two miles from the nearest part of it. We would strike it about halfway between Garland and Mantua, and we thought it just possible we would find passing along it some refugees from the two towns. I couldn't quite see how meeting them could help us any, unless we encountered some vehicle that would give us a lift. However, the walking would be easier, and when we got to the road we could decide which way to go—north to Frannie, or south around Garland to Powell.

The sun was just rising when we started again. It took us nearly an hour to reach the road. As far as we could see it was deserted. We stopped here and held another consultation.

"It's easily twelve miles up to Frannie," I said, "and I don't believe more than eight to Powell. Let's go that way. We can get down to Cody from there. I guess there are still people left in Powell."

We started down the road toward Garland. It seemed the sensible thing to do. We were both famished by now and thirsty also. I had an idea that, since the fires in Garland were about burned out, there might be an isolated house unharmed, where we could find food and water.

I sometimes wonder now at our temerity in venturing so calmly to face this unknown danger. We were in the enemy's country—an enemy whose methods of attacking us might at any moment prove a hundred times more efficacious than they had so far. But we did not consider that then.

There was, indeed, nothing else we could have done advantageously. This road we were on was the only one within twenty or thirty miles. To have struck west from our wrecked plane—away from the Mercutians—would have brought us to face a hundred miles or more of desert over to the Yellowstone.

It was now broad daylight—and almost cloudless, as is usual in this locality. Half an hour of walking brought us nearly to the outskirts of Garland. There was less smoke all the time. We judged the fire must be pretty well burned out by now. Behind us the smoke of Mantua, a much larger town than Garland, rose in a great rolling cloud.

We were walking along, wondering what we should find ahead, when suddenly behind Garland and off to the right we saw another huge cloud of smoke rising.

"Powell!" ejaculated Mercer, coming to a dead stop in the road. "Good God, they've got Powell, too!"

There was no doubt about it—the town of Powell was also in flames. We sat down together then at the side of the road. We didn't quite know what else to do. We were both faint. Our situation seemed every moment to be getting worse; we appeared further from even comparative safety now than when we left our plane at dawn.

There seemed nothing else to do now but go ahead into Garland, a distance of only half a mile. There we might find food and water; and, thus refreshed, we could start back north to cover the fifteen miles to Frannie.

Garland, a few days before, was a town of about five hundred inhabitants; but I do not suppose that, at the time of its destruction, there were more than a score or two of people remaining in it.

We started off again, and within twenty minutes were among the smoldering houses of the town. It consisted practically of only one street—the road we were on—with the houses strung along it. The houses had been, most of them, small frame structures. They were nothing now but smoldering heaps of ashes with the chimneys left standing, like gaunt, silent sentinels. As we passed on down the road we saw several twisted forms that we took for the remains of human beings. It is unnecessary for me to describe them. We hurried on, shuddering.

Our objective was the lower end of the town, for there, perhaps a quarter of a mile off to one side with a branch road leading to it, we saw a single house and out -buildings left standing. We turned down this road and approached the house. It was a rather good -looking building of the bungalow type with a wide -spreading porch. Beside it stood a long, low, rectangular building we took to be a garage. There was an automobile standing in the doorway, and behind it we caught the white gleam of an airplane wing.

"We're all right now," cried Mercer. "There's a car, and there's a plane inside. One of them ought to run."

At this unexpected good fortune we were jubilant. We could get back to Billings now in short order.

We climbed up the porch steps and entered the house. We did not call out, for it seemed obvious that no one would be there after what had occurred in Garland so near by.

"There must be something to eat here," I said. "Let's find out—and then get back to Billings."

The big living room was empty, but there was no sign of disorder. A closed door stood near at hand.

"That might be the way to the kitchen," I suggested. "Come on."

I pushed open the door and entered, with Mercer close behind me. It was a bedroom. The bed stood over by a window. I stopped in horror, for on the bed, hunched forward in a sitting position, was the body of a man!

With the first sudden shock of surprise over, we stopped to note details. The man's hand, lying on the blanket, clutched a revolver. A mirror directly across from him was shattered as though by a bullet. A small bedroom chair was overturned near the center of the room.

"He—he isn't burned." Mercer spoke the words hardly above a whisper. "Something else killed him—there's been a fight. They—"

He stopped.

A sudden panic seized me. I wanted to run—to do something—anything—that would get me away from the nameless, silent terror that seemed all about.

"Come on," I whispered back. "God! Let's get out of here."

THE FIRE PEOPLE

As we got out into the living room we heard slow, dragging footsteps on the porch outside. We stopped again, shrinking back against the wall.

"They—they—it's—" Mercer's whispered words died away. We were both terrified beyond the power of reasoning. The dragging footsteps came closer—a sound that had in it nothing of human tread. Then we heard soft voices—words that were unintelligible.

"It's the Mercutians," I found voice to whisper. "They—"

A figure appeared in the porch doorway, outlined against the light behind—the figure of a short, squat man. He seemed to have on some sort of white, furry garment. He was bareheaded, with hair falling to his shoulders.

At the sight of him my terror suddenly left me. Here was an enemy I could cope with. The dread fear of supernatural beings that had possessed me evaporated.

With a shout to Mercer I dashed forward directly at the doorway. I think the Mercutian had not yet seen us; he stood quite still, his body blocking the full width of the doorway.

I let fly with my fist as I came up and hit him full in the face. At the same instant my body struck his. He toppled backward and I went through the doorway. I tripped over him on the porch outside and fell sprawling. Before I could rise three other Mercutians fell upon me and pinned me down.

Mercer was right behind me in the doorway. I saw him pause an instant to see what was happening. There seemed to be five Mercutians altogether. The one I had hit lay quite still. Three others were holding me.

The fifth stood to one side, watching Mercer, but apparently inactive.

I saw Mercer hesitate. An expression of surprise came over his face. His body swayed; he took a single step forward, half turned, and then fell in a crumpled heap.

MIELA

The girl stood quiet beside the tree, watching Alan as he tied up his boat. She continued smiling. Alan stood up and faced her. He wondered what he should say—whether she could understand him any better than he could her.

"You speak English?" he began hesitantly.

The girl did not answer at once; she seemed to be trying to divine his meaning. Then she waved her hand—a curious movement, which he took to be a gesture of negation—her broadening smile disclosing teeth that were small, even, and very white.

At this closer view Alan could see she was apparently about twenty years old, as time is reckoned on earth. Her body was very slender, gracefully rounded, yet with an appearance of extreme fragility. Her slenderness, and the long, sleek wings behind, made her appear taller than she really was; actually she was about the height of a normal woman of our own race.

Her legs were covered by a pair of trousers of some silky fabric, grayish blue in color. Her bare feet were incased in sandals, the golden cords of which crossed her insteps and wound about her ankles, fastening down the lower hems of the trousers. A silken, gray-blue scarf was wound about her waist; crossing in front, it passed up over her breast and shoulders, crossing again between the wings behind and descending to the waist.

Her hair was a smooth, glossy black. It was parted in the middle, covered her ears, and came forward over each shoulder. The plaits were bound tightly around with silken cords; each was fastened to her body in two places, at the waist and, where the plait ended, the outside of the trouser leg just above the knee.

Her skin was cream colored, smooth in texture, and with a delicate flush of red beneath the surface. Her eyes were black, her face small and oval, with a delicately pointed chin. There was nothing remarkable about her features except that they were extraordinarily beautiful. But—and this point Alan noticed at once—there was in her expression, in the delicacy of her face, a spiritual look that he had never seen in a woman before. It made him trust her; and—even then, I think—love her, too.

Such was the strange girl as Alan saw her that morning standing beside the tree on the bank of the little Florida bayou.

"I can't talk your language," said Alan. He realized it was a silly thing to say. But his smile answered hers, and he went forward until he was standing close beside

29

her. She did not appear so tall now, for he towered over her, the strength and bigness of his frame making hers seem all the frailer by contrast.

He held out his hand. The girl looked at it, puzzled.

"Won't you shake hands?" he said; and then he realized that, too, was a silly remark.

She wrinkled up her forehead in thought; then, with a sudden comprehension, she laughed—a soft little ripple of laughter—and placed her hand awkwardly in his.

As he released her hand she reached hers forward and brushed it lightly against his cheek. Alan understood that was her form of greeting. Then she spread her wings and curtsied low—making as charming a picture, he thought, as he had ever seen in his life.

As she straightened up her eyes laughed into his, and again she spoke a few soft words—wholly unintelligible. Then she pointed toward the sun, which was still low over the horizon, and then to the silver object lying back near the center of the island.

"I know," said Alan. "Mercury."

The girl repeated his last word immediately, enunciating it almost perfectly. Then she laid her hand upon her breast, saying: "Miela."

"Alan," he answered, indicating himself.

The girl laughed delightedly, repeating the word several times. Then she took him by the hand and made him understand that she wished to lead him back into the island.

They started off, and then Alan noticed a curious thing. She walked as though weighted to the ground by some invisible load. She did not raise her feet normally, but dragged them, like a diver who walks on land in his heavily weighted iron shoes. After a few steps she spread her wings, and, flapping them slowly, was able to get along better, although it was obvious that she could not lift her body off the ground to fly.

For a moment Alan was puzzled, then he understood. The force of gravity on earth was too great for the power of her muscles, which were developed only to meet the pull of Mercury—a very much smaller planet.

The girl was so exceedingly frail Alan judged she did not weigh, here on earth, much over a hundred pounds. But even that he could see was too much for her. She could not fly, and it was only by the aid of her wings that she was able to walk with anything like his own freedom of movement.

He made her understand, somehow, that he comprehended her plight. Then, after a time, he put his left arm about her waist. She spread the great red wings out behind him, the right one passing over his shoulder; and in this fashion they went forward more easily.

The girl kept constantly talking and gesturing. She seemed remarkably intelligent; and even then, at the very beginning of their acquaintanceship, she made Alan understand that she intended to learn his language. Indeed, she seemed concerned about little else; and she went about her task systematically and with an ability that amazed him.

As they walked forward she kept continually stooping to touch objects on the ground—a stick, a handful of sand, a woodland flower, or a palmetto leaf. Or, again, she would indicate articles of his clothing, or his features. In each case Alan gave her the English word; and in each case she repeated it after him.

Once she stopped stock still, and with astonishing rapidity and accuracy rattled off the whole list—some fifteen or twenty words altogether—pointing out each object as she enunciated the word.

Alan understood then—and he found out afterward it was the case—that the girl's memory was extraordinarily retentive, far more retentive than is the case with any normal earth person. He discovered also, a little later, that her intuitive sense was highly developed. She seemed, in many instances, to divine his meaning, quite apart from his words or the gestures—which often were unintelligible to her—with which he accompanied them.

After a time they reached the Mercutian vehicle. It was a cubical box, with a pyramid-shaped top, some thirty feet square at the base, and evidently constructed of metal, a gleaming white nearer like silver than anything else Alan could think of. He saw that it had a door on the side facing him, and several little slitlike windows, covered by a thick, transparent substance which might have been glass.

As they got up close to it Alan expected the girl's companions to come out. His heart beat faster. Suddenly he raised his voice and shouted: "Hello, inside!"

The girl looked startled. Then she smiled and made the negative gesture with her hand.

Alan understood then that she was alone. They went inside the vehicle. It was dark in there. Alan could make out little, but after a moment his eyes grew accustomed to the darkness.

He noticed first that the thing was very solidly constructed. He expected to see some complicated mechanism, but there was little or nothing of the kind so far as he could make out in the darkness in this first hurried inspection.

Fastened to one wall was an apparatus which he judged was for the making of oxygen. He looked around for batteries, and for electric lights, but could see nothing of the kind.

All this time Alan's mind had been busily trying to puzzle out the mystery of the girl's presence here alone. Evidently she came in the most friendly spirit; and thus, quite evidently, her mission, whatever it was, must be very different from that of the invaders who had landed almost simultaneously in Wyoming.

Whatever it was that had brought her—whatever her purpose—he realized it must be important. The girl, even now, seemed making no effort to show or explain anything to him, but continued plying him with questions that gave her the English words of everything about them that she could readily indicate.

Alan knew then that she must have something important to communicate—something that she wanted to say as quickly as possible. And he knew that she realized the only way was for her to learn his language, which she was doing with the least possible loss of time, and with an utter disregard of everything else that might have obtruded.

Alan decided then to take the girl back home with him—indeed, it had never been in his mind to do anything else—and let Beth care for her. Meanwhile he would do everything he could to help her get the knowledge necessary to make known what it was that had brought her from Mercury. That she had some direct connection with the Wyoming invaders he did not doubt.

Alan had just reached this decision when the girl made him realize that she had the same thought in mind. She pointed around the room and then to herself, and he knew that she was insisting upon a general word to include all her surroundings.

Finally Alan answered: "House."

After pointing to him, she waved her hand vaguely toward the country outside the open doorway, and he understood she was asking where his house was.

Alan's decision was given promptly. "We'll go there," he said.

He put his arm about her and started out. By the way she immediately responded he knew she understood, and that it was what she wished to do.

They got back to Alan's launch in a few moments. He seated her in the stern of the boat, where she half reclined with her wings spread out a little behind her. So assiduous was she—and so facile—in her task of learning English, that before she would let him start the motor she had learned the names of many of the new objects in sight, and several verbs connected with his actions of the moment.

There was a large tarpaulin in the launch, and this Alan wrapped about the girl's shoulders. He did not want her vivid red wings to be seen by any one as they passed down the bayou.

Finally they started off.

Professor Newland's home was some three miles from the village of Bay Head, on the shore of a large bay which opened into the Gulf of Mexico. The bayou down which they were heading flowed into this bay near where the house stood. Their home was quite isolated, Alan thought with satisfaction. There was no other habitation nearer than Bay Head except a few negro shacks. With the girl's wings covered he could take her home and keep her there, in absolute seclusion, without causing any comment that might complicate things.

On the way down the bayou the girl showed extreme interest in everything about her. She seemed to have no fear, trusting Alan implicitly in his guidance and protection of her in this strange world. She continued her questions; she laughed frequently, with almost a childlike freedom from care. Only once or twice, he noticed, as some thought occurred to her, the laughter died away, her face suddenly sobered, and a far -away, misty look came into her beautiful eyes.

Alan sat close beside her in the stern, steering the launch and occasionally pulling the tarpaulin back onto her shoulders when it threatened to slip off because of her impetuous gestures.

They saw only a few negroes as they passed down the bayou, and these paid no particular attention to them. Within an hour Alan had the girl safely inside the bungalow, and was introducing her, with excited explanations, to his astonished father and sister, who were just at that moment sitting down to breakfast.

THE MERCUTIAN CAMP

As I saw Mercer fall to the floor of the porch a sudden rage swept over me. I struggled violently with the three men pinning me down. They appeared very much weaker than I, but even though I could break their holds the three of them were more than a match for me.

The man who was standing inactive, and who I realized had struck down Mercer in some unknown, deadly way, appeared to be the leader. Once, as one of my assailants made some move, the import of which the leader evidently understood, but which I did not, I heard him give a sharp command. It occurred to me then that if I offered too much resistance—if it seemed I was likely to get away from them—I might possibly be struck as swiftly as Mercer had been. So I gave up abruptly and lay still.

They must have understood my motive—or perhaps they felt that I was not worth the trouble of taking alive—for immediately I stopped struggling they unhanded me and rose to their feet.

I stood up also, deciding to appear quite docile, for the time being at any rate, until I could comprehend better with what I had to contend.

The man who appeared to be their leader issued another command. One of the men with whom I had been struggling immediately stepped a few feet away, out of my reach. I knew he had been told to guard me. He kept just that distance away thereafter, following my movements closely and seeming never to take his eyes off me for a moment.

I had opportunity now to inspect these strange enemies more closely. The leader was the tallest. He was about five and a half feet in height, I judged, and fairly stocky. The others were all considerably shorter—not much over five feet, perhaps. All were broad-framed, although not stout to any degree approaching fatness.

From their appearance, they might all have been fairly powerful men, the leader especially. But even the short struggle I had had with them showed me they were not. Their bodies, too, had seemed under my grip to have a flimsy quality, a lack of firmness, of solidity, entirely belied by their appearance.

They were all dressed in a single rude garment of short white fur, made all in one piece, trousers and shirt, and leaving only their arms bare. Their feet were incased in buskins that seemed to be made of leather. Their hair was a reddish-brown color, and fell scraggling a little below the shoulder line.

34

Their skin was a curious, dead white—like the pallor of a man long in prison. Their faces, which had no sign of hair on them, were broad, with broad flat noses, and with abnormally large eyes that seemed to blink stolidly with an owl-like stare.

Their leader was of somewhat different type. He was, as I have said, nearly six inches taller than the others, and leaner and more powerful looking. His hair was black, and his skin was not so dead white. His eyes were not so abnormally large as those of his companions. His nose was straight, with a high bridge. His face was hairless. It was a strong face, with an expression of dignity about it, a consciousness of power, and a certain sense of cruelty expressed in the firmness of his lips and the set of his chin.

None of them was armed—or, at least, their weapons were not visible to me.

I was much concerned about Mercer. He and the man I had hit were both lying motionless where they had fallen. I stooped over Mercer. No one offered to stop me, although when I moved I saw my guard make a swift movement with his hand to his belt. My heart leaped to my throat, but nothing happened to me, and I made a hasty examination of Mercer.

Quite evidently he was dead.

Meanwhile the Mercutians were examining their fallen comrade. He also was dead, I judged from their actions. They left him where he was lying, and their leader impatiently signed me toward the steps that led down from the porch to the roadway. We started off, my guard keeping close behind me. I noticed then how curiously hampered the Mercutians seemed to be in their movements.

I have explained how Alan observed the effect of our earth's gravity on Miela. It was even more marked with the Mercutians here, for she had the assistance of wings, while they did not. The realization of this encouraged me tremendously. I knew now that physically these enemies were no match for me; that I could break away from them whenever I wished.

But the way in which Mercer had been killed—that I could not understand. It was that I had to guard against. I was afraid to do anything that would expose me to this unknown attack.

I tried to guess over how great a distance this weapon, whatever it was, would prove effective. I assumed only a limited number of feet, although my only reason for thinking so was my guard's evident determination to keep close to me.

All this flashed through my mind while we were descending the steps to the roadway. When we reached the ground we turned back toward the garage, and with slow, plodding steps the leader of the Mercutians preceded me to its entrance, his companions following close behind me. They had evidently been here before, I could tell from their actions. I realized that probably they had all been inside the garage when Mercer and I first approached the house.

It was quite apparent now that the Mercutians did not understand the use of either automobiles or airplanes; they poked around these as though they were some strange, silent animals. Inside the garage I was ordered to stand quiet, with my guard near by, while the rest of them continued what appeared to be a search about the building.

We passed by the house, and I realized that we were starting for the Mercutian base some four miles away. I remembered then that I was extremely hungry and thirsty. I stopped suddenly and endeavored to explain my wants, indicating the house as a place where I could get food.

The leader smiled. His name was Tao, I had learned from hearing his men address him. I do not know why that smile reassured me, but it did. It seemed somehow to make these enemies less inhuman—less supernatural—in my mind. Indeed, I was fast losing my first fear of them, although I still had a great respect for the way in which they had killed Mercer.

Tao told his men to wait, and motioned me toward the house. The bodies of Mercer and the man I had struck down were still lying where they had fallen on the porch. We found food and water in the kitchen, and I sat down and made a meal, while Tao stood watching me. When I had finished I put several slices of bread and meat in my coat. He signified that it was unnecessary, but I insisted, and he smiled again and let me have my way.

Again we started off. This walk of four miles of desert that lay between Garland and the point on the Shoshone River where the invaders were established was about all I could manage, for I was almost exhausted. I realized then how great an exertion the Mercutians were put to, for they seemed nearly as tired as I. We stopped frequently to rest, and it was well after noon when we approached the hollow through which the Shoshone River ran.

Several times I noticed where the Mercutian Light had burned off the scrubby desert vegetation. As we got closer I could see it now in the sunlight, standing vertically up in the air, motionless. There were signs all about now where the light had burned. We were passing along a little gully—the country here was somewhat rough and broken up—when something came abruptly from behind a rock. Its extraordinary appearance startled me so I stared at it in amazement and fear. It came closer, and I saw it was one of the Mercutians.

He was completely incased in a suit of dull black cloth, or rubber, or something of the kind. On his head was a helmet of the same material, with a mask over his face having two huge circular openings covered with a flexible, transparent substance. On his back was a sort of tank with a pipe leading to his mouth. He looked, indeed, something like a man in a diving suit, and still more like the pictures I had seen of soldiers in the World War with gas masks on. He pulled off his helmet as he came up to us, and I saw he was similar in appearance to the red -haired Mercutians who had captured me.

After a short conversation with Tao he went back to his station by the rock, and we proceeded onward down the gully to the river bank. I saw a number of Mercutians dressed this way during the afternoon. They seemed to be guarding the approaches to the camp, and I decided later this costume was for protection against the effects of the light -ray.

The Shoshone River was at this point about two hundred feet wide, and at this season of the year a swift -moving, icy stream some two or three feet deep. There were small trees at intervals along its banks. All about me now I could see where they had been burned by the action of the light.

The vehicle in which the invaders had arrived lay on the near side of the river, some five hundred feet below where we came out of the gully. It was similar in appearance to the one Alan had found in Florida, only many times larger. It lay there now, with its pyramid -shaped top pointing up into the air, close beside the river, and gleaming a dazzling white under the rays of the afternoon sun.

There were perhaps a hundred Mercutians in sight altogether. Most of them were down by the vehicle; all of them were on this side of the river. In fact, as I soon realized, it would have been difficult, if not impossible, for them to have crossed. The desert on the opposite side of the Shoshone was level and unbroken. It was swept clear of everything, apparently, by the light -ray.

We turned down the river bank, and soon were close to the shining vehicle that had brought these strange invaders from space. What would I see in this camp of the first beings to reach earth from another planet? What fate awaited me there? These questions hammered at my brain as we approached the point where so much death and destruction had been dealt out to the surrounding country.

THE ESCAPE

The Mercutians all regarded me curiously as we came among them. By the respect they accorded Tao, and his attitude toward them, I decided he was the leader of the entire party. I stopped, wondering what would happen next. The man guarding me was still close at hand. Tao spoke a few words to him and then moved away. My guard immediately sat down. I saw nothing was required of me at the moment, and sat down also.

I had opportunity now to examine the strange things and people about me more in detail. The Mercutians all seemed to be of the same short, squat, red-haired type. Tao was, indeed, the only one I saw who had black hair; and he was the tallest, and by far the most commanding looking figure of them all.

They wore several different costumes, although the garment of white fur was the most common. A few were dressed in the black costume of the guard in the gully. Still others were garbed only in short, wide trousers and shirts of a soft leather, with legs bare from the knee down, and with leather buskins on their feet.

The light-ray was set up near the river, on a metallic structure supporting a small platform some thirty feet above the ground. A ladder up one side gave access to this platform from below. The light itself came from a cubical metallic box, perhaps six feet square, suspended above the platform in a balancing mechanism that allowed it to swing in all directions.

All the metal of this apparatus, the projector, the platform and its framework, was apparently of the same kind; it had the appearance of burnished copper. The whole seemed fairly complicated, but not unlike a huge search-light would appear if mounted that way.

Coming out of the projector and running down to the ground were black wires, which led to a metallic box a few feet away. This box was rectangular in shape; six feet long, perhaps, two feet broad, and the same in depth. I judged it to be the dynamo or battery from which the projector was supplied with the light-ray.

A short distance back from the river I saw what appeared to be a small mortar, which I assumed was for the sending of the light-rockets, or bombs. Several other light-ray projectors, sections of their supporting structures, and the unassembled parts of other apparatus, were lying scattered about the ground. A considerable number of the Mercutians were laboriously bringing out of the vehicle still more apparatus.

It was obvious to me then that they were only just getting started in their offensive and defensive preparations. This I could easily understand when I had watched for a moment the activities going on. All of the apparatus which they were engaged in bringing out and assembling was of metal, and it was so extremely heavy here on earth that they could hardly handle it.

Standing on the platform beside the light -ray projector were two men evidently in charge of it at the moment. They were dressed in black, with black gloves, although without helmets. I noticed that they had little pads over their ears, with wires running from them down to a small box at the waist.

Once I saw one of them look up sharply, as though he had heard something; and, following the wave of his hand, I saw the tiny black-garbed figure of a man on the higher ground behind the gully through which we had come. I reasoned then that this was a lookout stationed there, and that he was directing the action of the light by some form of wireless telephony.

For perhaps an hour I sat there, with my guard near by watching me. I was sorry, now that I found myself in the midst of these enemies, that I had not made a determined effort to escape earlier in the day, when there would have been only four of them to cope with.

I realized that I didn't know any more now about the power this guard had over me than I had at the beginning. He certainly looked inoffensive, sitting there, but the very calmness with which he watched me made me feel I would be taking a desperate chance in attempting to escape. I decided then to wait until nightfall and to watch a favorable opportunity to break away.

Under cover of darkness, if once I could get out of their sight, I was satisfied they would never catch me. It was my plan to strike back to Garland. I had noticed carefully the lay of the land coming over, and believed I could find my way back. Then, with the car or the plane that was there in the garage, I could get back to Billings.

These thoughts were running through my mind when Tao abruptly presented himself before me and ordered me to get up. I did so, smiling in as friendly a fashion as I could manage. He then made me assist in the work of carrying the heavy pieces of apparatus. Apparently he was determined that I, as an earth man, should work hard, since the Mercutians were so heavily handicapped by the gravity of my planet. I concluded that it would be my best policy to help them all I could—that by so doing they might relax a little in their watchfulness, and thus enable me to get away that night.

I signified to Tao my understanding of what he was after, and made them all see my entire readiness and ability to help. For the rest of the afternoon I was dragging about from place to place, carrying the projectors to the various positions where they had decided to put them up. It seemed to be their plan to establish some twenty or thirty projectors around the vehicle; they were setting them all at points about a hundred yards away from it. These projectors differed in size and shape. Some were cubical, others pyramid -shaped, open at the base as though to send out the light in a spreading ray.

I saw now, when I had a chance to inspect the projectors closer, that they were black outside and like burnished copper inside, to reflect the light. I judged that this black covering must have been like the black suits worn by some of the men, and that it was impervious to the light -ray. Near the center of each projector was a coil of wire. The wires from outside ran to it, and across the open face of the projector a large number of fine lateral wires ran parallel, very close together.

These were about all the details I noticed. I wanted to remember them, although they conveyed very little to me, because I realized all this I was seeing might prove of immense help to the authorities when I got back to Billings.

Night came, and I was still at work. Tao seemed tremendously pleased at what I was doing, and I noticed with satisfaction that his attitude toward me seemed gradually changing. My guard still followed me about, but he did not watch me quite so closely now, I thought.

My help, that afternoon, was considerable. I was by far the strongest man in the camp; and, more than that, I was able to move about so much faster than they that I could do things in a few moments that would have taken them many times as long.

Tao personally directed most of my efforts. He told me where to take the things, and I took them, smilingly, and always coming back to him for new orders. I moved so fast, indeed, that my guard had difficulty in keeping close to me. Several times I experimented and found that I could get away from him quite a little distance without a protest, either from him or from Tao.

As it began to grow dark, they lighted up the camp. This was accomplished by little metallic posts that had been set around at intervals. Each had a tiny coil of wire suspended at its top, which became incandescent and threw out a reddish -

green light. Around each light was a square black wire cage some three feet in diameter. I conjectured that these lights used the same ray as the projectors, only in a different form, and that the cage was to protect any one from going too close. The light from these illuminators was much the same in aspect as the ray, except that it seemed to diffuse itself readily and carried only a comparatively short distance.

The scene now, under this red-green glare, was weird in the extreme. The work all about me went on steadily. The Mercutians were all dressed in white furry garments now—I concluded because of the cold—with the exception of those who had on the suits and helmets of black.

The reddish-green light made them all appear like little gnomes at work. Indeed, the whole scene, with its points of color in the darkness, and the huge monstrous shadows all about, was more like some fantastic picture out of a fairy book than a scene on this earth.

Soon after nightfall Tao stopped me, and one of his men brought me something to eat. I still had the slices of bread and meat in my pocket, but, thinking I might need them later on, I kept them there. Tao and I sat down near one of the lights and ate together. We were served by one of the men. My guard still kept close at hand.

The food was nothing more than hard pieces of baked dough and a form of sweet something like chocolate. For drink there was a hot liquid quite comparable to tea. This was served us in small metal cups with handles that seemed to be insulated from the heat.

This meal was brought to us from inside the vehicle. While we were eating I could see many of the Mercutians going inside and coming out with pieces of this food in their hands, eating as they worked. Quite obviously the business of assembling their apparatus was uppermost in the minds of all of them.

The whole atmosphere about the place, I realized now, in spite of the opposite effect their dragging footsteps gave, was one of feverish activity. When we had eaten Tao seemed willing to sit quiet for a while. My efforts to talk to him amused us both greatly, and I noticed with satisfaction that he seemed to trust me more and more.

Finally my guard spoke, asking permission, I judged, to leave us and go have his dinner. My heart leaped into my throat as I saw him go, leaving me alone with Tao. I concluded that now, if ever, was my opportunity. Tao trusted me—seemed to like me, in fact. No one else in the camp was paying the least attention to us. If only I could, on some pretext, get myself a reasonable distance away from him I would make a run for it.

I was turning this problem over in my mind when it was unexpectedly solved for me. A low throbbing, growing momentarily louder, sounded from the air—the hum of an airplane motor. I think Tao noticed it first—I saw him cock his head to one side, listening.

After a moment, as the sound increased, he climbed to his feet and shouted an order to the man nearest us.

The night had clouded over; it was unusually dark. I knew that a plane without lights was approaching. Work about the camp stopped; every one stood listening. I looked up at the light-ray platform. The two men there were swinging the light back and forth, sweeping the sky.

Suddenly the sound ceased; the plane's motor had been shut off. Almost at the same instant the light-ray picked up the plane. It was several thousand feet in the air and almost over our heads, coming down in a spiral. A moment more and the light-ray swung away.

The plane burst into flame, and I knew it was falling. An explosion sounded near at hand. The camp was in chaos immediately. I faced about to look at Tao; he had disappeared.

I waited no longer. Turning back from the river, I ran at full speed.

FUTILE ATTACKS

There seemed to be no pursuit. In a few moments I was clear of the camp and hidden in the darkness of the desert. I ran perhaps half a mile, then I slowed down to a walk, completely winded. Turning, I could see behind me the lights of the camp. I doubted if even now they had missed me. The bomb dropped by the airplane and the plane itself falling almost, in their midst must have plunged them for the time into confusion.

I kept on walking rapidly. The desert here was almost pathless; occasionally I would cross a wandering wagon track, but none of them seemed going in my direction. After a time I was not sure what my direction was; all about me was a luminous darkness—and silence.

I found myself now almost exhausted from my exertions of the day. I decided to go possibly a mile farther—to be well away from the Mercutians—and then to lie down and sleep until daylight.

In about fifteen minutes more I concluded I had gone far enough, and, lying down on the sand, was soon fast asleep. When I awoke it was daylight, with the sun just rising.

With returning consciousness I looked about me in sudden fear, but there was no one in sight. I ate the bread and meat I had in my pocket, and, feeling much refreshed, but thirsty, I started again for Garland.

I made the town soon after noon that day. The little automobile was still standing in the garage, and I started it without trouble. Before I left I went up to the porch of the house.

The bodies of Mercer and the Mercutian were still lying there. I dragged Mercer's body down the steps and put it into the back seat of the car Then I started off. I stuck to the main road, and went through Mantua at top speed, apprehensive that some of the Mercutians might be there. This town, like Garland, was completely burned. Only the chimneys were left standing amid piles of ashes.

At Frannie I took on two passengers. There was much curiosity on the part of those I met along here, but I was unwilling to explain, deciding it best to wait and tell my whole story to the military authorities at Billings.

It was early afternoon when I got back to Billings. This was March 12. I turned Mercer's body over to the police, who promptly took me in charge. I gave them a brief outline of what had occurred. General Price, whose command of the United

THE FIRE PEOPLE

States military operations against the Mercutians was announced to the country two days later, had arrived that morning in Billings by airplane. I demanded to see him, and when my business was explained to him he granted me an immediate interview.

General Price was a man about fifty, a kindly gentleman of the old Southern type, yet of thoroughly military demeanor. I told him everything that had happened to me in detail as complete as I possibly could. Mercer's body was examined that same afternoon. It was found to have been drilled completely through the chest by a hole about the diameter of a lead pencil. This hole did not seem to have been made by the passage of any foreign object, but had more the aspect of a burn. I understood then—Mercer had been killed by a tiny light -ray projector, with a short, effective radius, aimed probably like a revolver.

What I was able to tell General Price about the Mercutians naturally was invaluable to him. He asked me then to remain close to him during the forthcoming operations. We arranged that I was on honor to give nothing out to my paper without his approval.

The situation, as it appeared during the next few days, was not one of grave danger. We were able to gage now with fair probability of correctness the offensive strength of our enemies. They had no means of transportation—could only move from their present position slowly and with extreme difficulty. The possibility of the vehicle itself moving occurred to us; but, as I pointed out, the task of replacing their heavy apparatus in it, and then reassembling the apparatus in a new position, made such a step impractical.

The only weapon the Mercutians had displayed so far was the light -ray in its several forms. This seemed effective for ten miles at most. That the Mercutians could be attacked by our artillery and destroyed seemed certain.

By the 20th General Price had mobilized some ten thousand men. They encamped on the prairie near Billings. The artillery was moved down to a point near the Wyoming State line, about fifteen miles directly north of the Mercutian camp.

Six days before this, forty -eight hours after I had returned to Billings, observation planes had reported the establishment of two more light -rays, similar in appearance to the first. During the succeeding days others rapidly appeared. By the 20th there were probably thirty of them altogether.

The reports stated that all were set up within a space seemingly of a few hundred yards. They were of different diameters; some projected in parallel rays, others

44

spread out fan -shaped. These latter appeared not to carry so far. The first one that had appeared, it was judged, had the longest effective radius of them all.

During these days and nights preceding the 20th the light -rockets had been fired with increasing frequency, but none was observed to carry over six or eight miles. By this time the burned area for a circle of ten miles all around the Mercutian camp was entirely depopulated, and no additional destruction was reported.

On the night of the 20th, firing by directions from captive balloons, the United States artillery began its bombardment from the Montana -Wyoming line. After sending over some twenty shells, the firing ceased. It was learned then that they had proven utterly ineffective. The diverging rays of the Mercutian light had thrown a barrage around their position. The shells striking the light had all exploded harmlessly in the air.

Subsequent bombardments made that night met with no better success. The fact became obvious then that to artillery fire the Mercutians were impregnable. For several days no further military operations were attempted, with the exception of an occasional shell futilely thrown against the light -rays.

The newspapers during these days were full of discussions—scientific and otherwise—as to how this strange enemy of mankind could be destroyed or dislodged. This was like no other warfare in history. The newspaper statements gave the inference that General Price was entirely at a loss how to proceed.

As a matter of fact, the press was quite correct in that assumption; and, since the Mercutians were making no offensive moves, General Price decided to do nothing until he was better informed.

I was fortunate enough to be present the next day at a conference the general had with several scientific men who had come to Billings to meet him. It was the opinion of these men of science that no artillery fire could penetrate the light - barrage the Mercutians had thrown about them. No airplane attack was practical, and to attack them from the ground with infantry would be absurd.

On the other hand, it seemed obvious that the Mercutians could make no offensive move either. They had probably already done all the damage that they could. If matters were allowed to remain as they now were—thus avoiding the useless sacrifice of men—inevitably the time would come when the food supply the Mercutians had brought with them would be exhausted. Meanwhile, if the invaders decided to move in their vehicle to another location, they could not do so suddenly without abandoning their apparatus.

THE FIRE PEOPLE

Any lessening in the number of light-rays in operation could be taken as an indication that a move of this kind was in preparation, and the warning would give General Price time to execute any attack that in the meantime might be planned.

It was decided then to remain comparatively inactive and await developments from the opposite side.

During the three months that followed this decision artillery bases were located at intervals on a circumference of about fifteen miles around the Mercutian center. These were all on desert country. Lines of communication between them were established, and the air above was thoroughly patrolled night and day.

The ten thousand men under General Price it was not thought necessary or advisable to augment. They were deployed around this circumference in front of the artillery, nearer the ten-mile limit. Machine-gun outposts, manned by volunteers exclusively, were established in Garland, Mantua and other points within the area controlled by the light. These were for the purpose of preventing, or reporting, any possible movements on foot of the Mercutians.

During this time the government was, naturally, subjected to much harsh criticism for its waiting attitude. It was suggested that armored tanks—relics of the World War—could be put into commission. These, under cover of darkness, could be used to rush the Mercutian position. This obviously was an absurd plan, since the light-ray would instantly raise the temperature of the metal composing the car to such a height that the men inside would be killed—not to mention the fact that all explosives in the car would be instantly detonated.

Another suggestion was that a night raid be made upon the outposts of the camp by a few men armed with machine guns fired from the shoulder, in an effort to capture one of the Mercutians garbed in a suit impervious to the light. With this suit even one man with a machine gun would probably be able to clean out the Mercutian camp.

This plan evoked much favorable comment. This black material, once in our possession, could be analyzed and possibly be duplicated in quantity by us. It seemed the logical way of making progress.

But, unfortunately, conditions around the Mercutian camp at present were not the same as that night when I escaped. At that time it would have been feasible; now it was impossible, for all the invaders were within the small circle of projectors, and the ground outside this circle was never free from the diverging rays of the light. Also, as one newspaper article replied, even with such a suit of armor a man with a machine gun could do little, for the light would instantly render useless the gun itself.

So the controversy went on, and General Price waited, knowing that each day must bring the enemy nearer starvation. Such was the condition of affairs in the latter part of June.

Then, one morning, I received a telegram from Alan Newland in Florida. I had been corresponding with him at intervals, but he had never given me a hint of what had happened down there.

The telegram read:

Important Mercutian development here.

Keep absolutely secret. Join us here at once.

Answer.

I wired him immediately. Three days later I was at Bay Head.

MIELA'S STORY

When I reached the little Florida town Alan was there to meet me. He would have none of my eager questions, but took me at once by launch to their bungalow. No one was on the porch when we landed, and we went immediately into the living room. There I found Beth and Professor Newland talking to this extraordinary girl from another world, of whose existence, up to that moment, I had been in complete ignorance. She was dressed especially for my coming, they told me afterward, exactly as she had been that morning when Alan found her. They wanted to confound me, and they succeeded.

I stood staring in amazement while Beth quietly introduced me. And Miela spread her wings, curtsied, and replied in a quaint, soft little voice: "I am honored, sir." Then she laughed prettily and, extending her hand, added: "How do you do, Bob—my friend?"

When I had partially recovered from my astonishment Miela put on the big blue -cloth cape she wore constantly to cover her wings. Then Alan and Beth plunged into an excited explanation of how he had found Miela, and how all this time she had remained in seclusion with them there studying their language.

"You never have seen such assiduous young people," Professor Newland put in. "And certainly she has been a wonderful pupil."

He patted Miela's hand affectionately; but I noticed then that his eyes were very sad, as though from some unvoiced trouble or apprehension.

They had decided, the professor said, to keep the girl's presence a secret from the world until they had learned from her in detail what her mission was. The vehicle in which she had come was still on the island up the bayou. Alan had stationed there three young men of Bay Head whom he could trust. They were living on the island, guarding it.

During these two months while Miela, with uncanny rapidity, was mastering their language, the Newlands had of course learned from her all she had to tell them. The situation in Wyoming did not necessitate haste on their part, and so they had waited. And now, with a decision reached, they sent for me.

That evening after supper we all went out on the bungalow porch, and Miela told me her story. She spoke quietly, with her hands clasped nervously in her lap. At times in her narrative her eyes shone with the eager, earnest sincerity of her words; at others they grew big and troubled as she spoke of the problems that were harassing her world and mine—the inevitable self-struggles of humanity, whatever its environment, itself its own worst enemy.

"I am daughter of Lua," Miela began slowly, "of the Great City in the Country of Light. My mother, Lua, is a teacher of the people. My father, Thaal, died when still I was a child. I—I came to your earth—"

She paused and, turning to Beth, added appealingly:

"Oh, there is so much—to begin—how can I tell—"

"Tell him about Tao," Beth said.

"Tao!" I exclaimed.

"He leads those who came to your earth in the north," Miela went on. "He was my"—she looked to Alan for the word—"my suitor there in the Great City. He wished me for his wife—for the mother of his children. But that—that was not what I wished."

"You'd better tell him about conditions in your world first, Miela," said Alan. He spoke very gently, tenderly.

I had already seen, during supper, how he felt toward her; I could readily understand it, too, for, next to Beth, she seemed the most adorable woman I had ever met. There was nothing unusually strange about her, when her wings were covered, except her quaint accent and sometimes curious gestures; and no one could be with her long without feeling the sweet gentleness of her nature and loving her for it.

"Tell him about your women," Beth added.

I noticed the affectionate regard she also seemed to have for Miela; and I noticed, too, that there was in her face that vague look of sorrow that was in her father's.

The habitable world of Mercury, Miela then went on to tell me, was divided into three zones—light, twilight and darkness. There was no direct sunlight in the Light Country—only a diffused daylight like the light on our earth when the sky is clouded over. The people of the Light Country, Miela's people, were the most civilized and the ruling race.

In the twilight zone around them, grading back to the Dark Country, various other peoples dwelt, and occasionally warred with their neighbors for possession of land in the light.

In the center of the Light Country, directly underneath the sun—that is, where the sun, would always appear near the zenith—was the Fire Country. Here, owing to violent storms, the atmospheric envelope of the planet was frequently disturbed sufficiently to allow passage for the sun's direct rays. Then would ensue in that locality, for a limited time, a heat so intense as to destroy life. This Fire Country was practically uninhabited.

"You see, Bob," Alan interrupted, "the dark part of Mercury—that is the side that continually faces away from the sun—is also practically uninhabited. Only strange animals and savages live there. And the twilight zones, and the ring of Light Country, with the exception of its center, are too densely populated. This has caused an immense amount of trouble. The Twilight People are an inferior race. They have tried to mix with those of the Light Country. It doesn't work. There's been trouble for generations; trouble over the women, for one thing. Anyhow, the Twilight People have been kept out as much as possible. Now this fellow Tao—"

"Let Miela explain about the women first," Beth interjected.

Then Miela went on to tell me that only the females of Mercury had wings—given them by the Creator as a protection against the pursuit of the male. At marriage, to insure submission to the will of her husband, a woman's wings were clipped. For more than a generation now there had been a growing rebellion on the part of the women against this practice. In this movement Miela's mother, Lua, was a leader. To overcome this masculine desire for physical superiority and dominance which he had had for centuries seemed practically impossible. Yet, Miela said, the leaders of the women now felt that some progress was being made in changing public sentiment, although so far not a single man had been found who would take for mate a woman with wings unclipped.

This was partly from personal pride and partly because the laws of the country made such a union illegal, its parties moral outlaws, its children illegitimate, and thus not entitled to the government benefits bestowed upon all offspring of legitimate parentage. It was this man -made law the women were fighting, and of recent years fighting more and more militantly.

This was the situation when Tao suddenly projected himself into public affairs as the leader of a new movement. Tao had paid court to Miela without success. He was active in the fight against the woman movement—a brilliant orator, crafty, unscrupulous, a good leader. Leadership was to him purely a matter of personal gain. He felt no deep, sincere interest in any public movement for any other reason.

Interplanetary communication had become of latter years a possibility; science had invented and perfected the means. So far these vehicles had only been used for short trips to the outer edge of the atmosphere of Mercury—trips that were giving scientific men much valuable knowledge of atmospheric conditions, and which it was thought would ultimately enable them to counteract the storms and make the Fire Country habitable. No trips into space had been made.

Tao now came forward with the proposition to undertake a new world conquest—a conquest of Venus or the earth. These planets recently had been observed from the vehicles. This, he said, would solve the land question, which, after all, was more serious than the clipping of women's wings.

He found many followers—adventurers, principally, to whom the possibilities for untold personal gain in such a conquest appealed. Then abruptly the women took part. Dropping for the time their own fight, they opposed Tao vigorously. If Venus or the earth were inhabited, as it was thought they were, such an expedition would be a war against humanity. It would result in the needless destruction of human life.

In this controversy the government of the Light Country remained neutral. But the women finally won, and Tao and his followers, a number of them men of science, were all banished by the government, under pressure of popular sentiment, into the Twilight Country.

Here Tao's project fell upon fertile soil. The Twilight People had every reason to undertake such a conquest; and Tao became their leader in preparing for it. These preparations were known in the Light Country. The government made no effort to prevent them. It was, indeed, rather glad of the possibility of being rid of its disturbing neighbors.

Only the women were concerned, but they alone could do nothing, since by principle they were as much opposed to offensive warfare against the Twilight People as against the possible inhabitants of the earth. Miela paused at this point in her narrative. The thing was getting clearer to me now, but I could not reconcile this feeble attempt to conquer the earth which we were then fighting in Wyoming with the picture she drew. I said so.

"She hasn't come to that," Alan broke in. "You see, Bob, Tao, with about a hundred followers, was banished to the Twilight Country a couple of years ago. There was plenty of brains in the party, scientific men and such. They had only one vehicle, but they have been at work ever since building a lot of others.

"This expedition of Tao to Wyoming—with only about a hundred of the Twilight People with him—is not intended to be an offensive operation at all. He's only looking the situation over, finding out what they're up against. They decided before they started that the light-ray would protect them from anything on earth, and they have only come to look around.

"Right now up there"—Alan leaned forward earnestly, and in the moonlight I could see the flush on his handsome face—"right now up there in the Twilight Country of Mercury they're working their damnedest over all kinds of preparations. This Wyoming business this summer does not mean a thing Tao will quit it any minute. You'll see. Some morning we'll wake up and find them gone. Probably they'll destroy their apparatus, and not bother to take it back.

"And then, in a year or two, they'll be here again. Not one vehicle next time, but a hundred. They'll land all over the earth at once, not on a desert—Tao probably only picked that this time to avoid complications—but in our big cities, New York, Paris, London, all of them at once. That's what we've got to face.

"If Tao comes back as he plans, we have not got a chance. That's why Miela stole this little vehicle and, without it being publicly known in Mercury, came here to warn us. That's what she was after, to help us, risked her life to warn us people of another world."

Alan stopped abruptly, and, dropping to the floor of the porch beside Miela, laid his arm across her lap, looking up into her face as though she were a goddess. She stroked his hair tenderly, and I could see her eyes were wet with tears.

There was a moment's silence. I could not have known what Professor Newland and Beth were thinking, but a moment later I understood.

Then I realized the sorrow that was oppressing them both.

"What can be done?" I asked finally.

Alan jumped to his feet. He began pacing up and down the porch before us; evidently he was laboring under a great nervous excitement.

"There's nothing to be done," he said—"nothing at all—here on earth. We have not got a chance. It's up there the thing has got to be fought out—up there on Mercury—to keep them from returning."

Alan paused again. When he resumed his voice was pitched lower, but was very tense.

"I'm going there, Bob—with Miela."

I heard Professor Newland's sharply indrawn breath, and saw Beth's dear face suddenly whiten.

"I'm going there to fight it out with them. I may come back; I may not. But if I am successful, they never will—which is all that matters.

"Miela's mother gave her up to come down here and help us. It is a little thing to go back there to help us, also. If I can help her people with their own problems, so much the better."

He pulled Miela to her feet beside him and put his arm protectingly about her shoulders.

"And Miela is going back to her world as my wife—her body unmutilated—the first married woman in Mercury with wings as God gave them to her!"

TO SAVE THE WORLD

Two days later Alan and Miela were quietly married in Bay Head. She still wore the long cloak, and no one could have suspected she was other than a beautiful stranger in the little community. When we got back home Alan immediately made her take off the cloak. He wanted us to admire her wings—to note their long, soft red feathers as she extended them, the symbol and the tangible evidence of her freedom from male dominance.

She was as sweet about it all as she could be, blushing, as though to expose the wings, now that she was married, were immodest. And by the way she regarded Alan, by the gentleness and love in her eyes, I could see she would never be above the guidance, the dominance, of one man, at least.

The day before their marriage Alan had taken me up the bayou to see the little silver car in which Miela had come. I was intensely curious to learn the workings of this strange vehicle. As soon as we were inside I demanded that Alan explain it all to me in detail.

He smiled.

"That's the remarkable part of it, Bob," he answered. "Miela herself didn't thoroughly understand either the basic principle or the mechanism itself when she started down here."

"Good Lord! And she ventured—"

"Tao was already on the point of leaving when she conceived the idea. He had already made one trip almost to the edge of the earth's atmosphere, you know, and now was ready to start again."

"That first trip was last November," I said. "Tell me about that. What were those first light-meteors for?"

"As far as I can gather from what Miela says," Alan answered, "Tao wanted to make perfectly sure the light-ray would act in our atmosphere. He came—there were several vehicles they had ready even then—without other apparatus than those meteors, as we called them. Those he dropped to earth with the light-ray stored in them. They did discharge it properly—they seemed effective. The thing was merely a test. Tao was satisfied, and went back to arrange for this second preliminary venture in which he is engaged now."

"I understand," I said. "Go on about Miela."

"Well, she and her mother went before the Scientific Society, she calls it—the men who own and control these vehicles in the Light Country. They called it suicide. No one could be found to come with her. Lua, her mother, wanted to, but Miela would not let her take the risk, saying she was needed more there in her own world.

"As a matter of fact, the thing, while difficult perhaps to understand in principle, in operation works very simply. Miela knew that, and merely asked them to show her how to operate it practically. This they did. She spent two days with them—she learns things rather easily, you know—and then she was ready."

I waited in amazement.

"For practical purposes all she had to understand was the operation of these keys. The pressure of the light -ray in these coils"—he was standing beside a row of wire coils which in the semi -darkness I had not noticed before—"is controlled by the key -switches." He indicated the latter as he spoke. "They send a current to the outer metal plates of the car which makes them repel or attract other masses of matter, as desired.

"All that Miela had to understand then was how to operate these keys so as to keep the base of the vehicle headed toward the earth. They took her to the outer edge of the atmosphere of Mercury over the Dark Country and showed her the earth. They have used terrestrial telescopes for generations, and since the invention of this vehicle telescopes for celestial observation have been greatly improved.

"All Miela had to do was keep the air in here purified. That is a simple chemical operation. By using this attractive and repellent force she allowed the earth's gravity and the repelling power of the sun and Mercury to drive her here."

He paused.

"But, doesn't she—don't you understand the thing in detail?" I asked finally.

"I think father and I understand it now better than she does," he answered. "We have studied it out here and questioned her as closely as possible. We understand its workings pretty thoroughly. But the exact nature of the light -ray we do not understand, any more than we understand electricity. Nor do we understand this metallic substance which when charged with the current becomes attractive or repellent in varying degrees."

"Yes," I said. "That I can appreciate."

"Father has a theory about the light -ray," he went on, "which seems rather reasonable from what we can gather from Miela. The thing seems more like electricity than anything else, and father thinks now that it is generated by dynamos on Mercury, similar to those we use here for electricity."

"Along that line," I said, "can you explain why this light -ray, which will immediately set anything on fire that is combustible, and which acts through metal, like those artillery shells, for instance, does not seem to raise the temperature of the ground it strikes to any extent?"

"Because, like electricity, it is dissipated the instant it strikes the ground. The earth is an inexhaustible storehouse and receptacle for such a force. That is why the broken country around the Shoshone River protected Garland and Mantua from its direct rays."

"Tell me about the details of this mechanism," I said, reverting to our original subject. "You say you understand its workings pretty thoroughly now."

"Yes, I do," he admitted, "and so does father. But I cannot go into it now with you. You see," he added hastily, as though he feared to hurt my feelings, "the scientific men of Mercury—some of them—objected to Miela's coming, on the ground that the inhabitants of the earth, obtaining from her a knowledge that would enable them to voyage through space, might take advantage of that knowledge to undertake an invasion of Mercury.

"As a matter of fact, that was a remote possibility. I could explain to you all I know about this mechanism without much danger of your ever being able to build such a car. But Miela promised them that she would use all possible precautions, in the event of her having any choice in the matter, to prevent the earth people learning anything about it.

"Father and I have examined everything here closely. But no one else has—and I am sure Miela would prefer no one else did. You understand, Bob?"

I did understand; and of course I had to be satisfied with that.

"It seems to me," I said when, later in the day, we were discussing affairs in Wyoming, "that with things in Mercury as we now know they are, it would help the situation tremendously if Tao and these Twilight People with him were prevented from ever returning."

"That's my idea exactly," Professor Newland agreed.

I could see by the look on his face he was holding on to this thought as a possibility that might make Alan's plan unnecessary.

"I've thought about it constantly," the professor said, "ever since these facts first came to us through Miela. It would be important. With his expedition here a total failure, I think we might assume that nothing more would be done up there in attempting to conquer the earth. I've tried to make Alan see that we should give the authorities all the information we have. It might help—something might be accomplished—"

"Nothing would, father," Alan interrupted. "There wouldn't be time. And even if this expedition of Tao's were destroyed, I don't see why that's any guarantee another attempt would not be made. Miela doesn't, either, and she ought to know.

"Besides, don't you see, Bob"—he turned to me earnestly—"I can't have the eyes of the world turned on Miela and her affairs? Why, think of it—this little woman sent to Washington, questioned, photographed, written about, made sport of, perhaps, in the newspapers! And all for nothing. It is unthinkable."

"You may be right, my boy," said the professor sadly. "I am giving in to you, but I still—"

"The thing has come to me," said Alan. "A duty—a responsibility put squarely up to me. I've accepted it. I'll do my best all the way."

A week after Alan and Miela were married the report came that the Mercutians had suddenly departed, abandoning, after partly destroying, their apparatus. The world for a few days was in trepidation, fearing a report that they had landed somewhere else, but no such report came.

Three days later Alan and Miela followed them into space.

Professor Newland, Beth and I went up the bayou with them that morning they left. We were a solemn little party, none of us seemingly wishing to voice the thoughts that possessed us all.

Professor Newland never spoke once during the trip. When the moment of final parting came he kissed Miela quietly, and, pressing Alan's hand, said simply: "Good luck, my boy. We appreciate what you are doing for us. Come back, some day, if you can."

Then he faced about abruptly and trudged back to the launch alone, as pathetic a figure as I have ever seen. We all exchanged our last good-bys, little Beth in tears clinging to Alan, and then kissing Miela and making her promise some day to come back with Alan when he had accomplished his mission.

Then they entered the vehicle. Its heavy door closed. A moment later it rose silently—slowly at first, then with increasing velocity until we could see it only as a little speck in the air above us. And then it was gone.

THE LANDING ON MERCURY

(Narrative continued by Alan Newland.)

With hardly more than a perceptible tremor our strange vehicle came to rest upon the surface of Mercury. For a moment Miela and I stood regarding each other silently. Then she left her station at the levers of the mechanism and placed her hands gently on my shoulders. "You are welcome, my husband, here to my world."

I kissed her glowing, earnest face. We had reached our journey's end. My work was about to begin—upon my own efforts now depended the salvation of that great world I had left behind. What difficulties, what dangers, would I have to face, here among the people of this strange planet? I thrilled with awe at the thought of it; and I prayed God then to hold me firm and steadfast to my purpose.

Miela must have divined my thoughts, for she said simply: "You will have great power here, Alan; and it is in my heart that you will succeed."

We slid back one of the heavy metallic curtains and looked out through the thick glass of the window. It was daylight—a diffused daylight like that of a cloudy midday on my own earth. An utterly barren waste met my gaze. We seemed to have landed in a narrow valley. Huge cliffs rose on both sides to a height of a thousand feet or more.

These cliffs, as well as the floor of the valley itself, shone with a brilliant glare, even in the half light of the sunless day. They were not covered with soil, but seemed rather to be almost entirely metallic, copper in color. The whole visible landscape was devoid of any sign of vegetation, nor was there a single living thing in sight.

I shuddered at the inhospitable bleakness of it.

"Where are we, Miela?"

She smiled at my tone. It was my first sight of Mercury except vague, distant glimpses of its surface through the mist coming down.

"You do not like my world?"

She was standing close beside me, and at her smiling words raised one of her glorious red wings and spread it behind me as though for protection. Then, becoming serious once more, she answered my question.

"We are fortunate, Alan. It is the Valley of the Sun, in the Light Country. I know it well. We are very close to the Great City."

I breathed a sigh of relief.

"I'll leave it all to you, little wife. Shall we start at once?"

Her hand pressed mine.

"I shall lead you now," she said. "But afterward—you it will be who leads me—who leads us all."

She crossed to the door fastenings. As she loosed them I remember I heard a slight hissing sound. Before I could reach her she slid back the door. A great wave of air rushed in upon us, sweeping us back against the wall. I clutched at something for support, but the sweep of wind stopped almost at once.

I had stumbled to my knees. "Miela!" I cried in terror.

She was beside me in an instant, wide-eyed with fear, which even then I could see was fear only for me.

I struggled to my feet. My head was roaring. All the blood in my body seemed rushing to my face.

After a moment I felt better. Miela pulled me to a seat.

"I did not think, Alan. The pressure of the air is different here from your world. It was so wrong of me, for I knew. It was so when I landed there on your earth."

I had never thought to ask her that, nor had she ever spoken of it to me. She went on now to tell me how, when first she had opened the door on that little Florida island, all the air about her seemed rushing away. She had felt then as one feels transported quickly to the rarified atmosphere of a great height.

Here the reverse had occurred. We had brought with us, and maintained, an air density such as that near sea level on earth. But here on Mercury the air was far denser, and its pressure had rushed in upon us instantly the door was opened. Miela had been affected to a much less extent than I, and in consequence recovered far more quickly.

The feeling, after the first nausea, the pressure and pain in my ears and the roaring in my head, had passed away. A sense of heaviness, an inability to breathe with accustomed freedom, remained with me for days.

We sat quiet for some minutes, and then left the vehicle. Miela was dressed now as I had first seen her on the Florida bayou. As we stepped upon the ground she suddenly tore the veil from her breast, spread her wings, and, with a laugh of sheer delight, flew rapidly up into the air. I stood watching her, my heart beating fast. Up—up she went into the gray haze of the sky. Then I could see her spread her great wings, motionless, a giant bird soaring over the valley.

THE FIRE PEOPLE

A few moments more, and she was again beside me, alighting on the tip of one toe with perfect poise and grace almost within reach of my hand.

I do not quite know what feelings possessed me at that moment. Perhaps it was a sense of loss as I saw this woman I loved fly away into the air while I remained chained to the ground. I cannot tell. But when she came back, dropping gently down beside me, ethereal and beautiful as an angel from heaven itself, a sudden rush of love swept over me.

I crushed her to me, glorying in the strength of my arms and the frailness of her tender little body.

When I released her she looked up into my eyes archly.

"You do not like me to fly? Your wife is free—and, oh, Alan, it is so good—so good to be back here again where I can fly."

She laughed at my expression.

"You are a man, too—like all the men of my world. That is the feeling you came here to conquer, Alan—so that the women here may all keep their wings—and be free."

I think I was just a little ashamed of myself for a moment. But I knew my feeling had been only human. I did want her to fly, to keep those beautiful wings. And in that moment they came to represent not only her freedom, but my trust in her, my very love itself.

I stroked their sleek red feathers gently with my hand.

"I shall never feel that way again, Miela," I said earnestly.

She laughed once more and kissed me, and the look in her eyes told me she understood.

The landscape, from this wider viewpoint, seemed even more bleak and desolate than before. The valley was perhaps half a mile broad, and wound away upward into a bald range of mountains in the distance.

The ground under my feet was like a richly metallic ore. In places it was wholly metal, smooth and shining like burnished copper. Below us the valley broadened slightly, falling into what I judged must be open country where lay the city of our destination.

For some minutes I stood appalled at the scene. I had often been in the deserts of America, but never have I felt so great a sense of desolation. Always before it had been the lack of water that made the land so arid; and always the scene seemed to hold promise of latent fertility, as though only moisture were needed to make it spring into fruition.

Nothing of the kind was evident here. There was, indeed, no lack of water. I could see a storm cloud gathering in the distance. The air I was breathing seemed unwarrantably moist; and all about me on the ground little pools remained from the last rainfall. But here there was no soil, not so much even as a grain of sand seemed to exist. The air was warm, as warm as a midsummer's day in my own land, a peculiarly oppressive, moist heat.

I had been prepared for this by Miela. I was bareheaded, since there never was to be direct sunlight. My feet were clad in low shoes with rubber soles. I wore socks. For the rest, I had on simply one of my old pairs of short, white running pants and a sleeveless running shirt. With the exception of the shoes it was exactly the costume I had worn in the races at college.

I had been standing motionless, hardly more than a step from the car in which we had landed. Suddenly, in the midst of my meditations on the strange scene about me, Miela said: "Go there, Alan."

She was smiling and pointing to a little rise of ground near by. I looked at her blankly.

"Jump, Alan," she added.

The spot to which she pointed was perhaps forty feet away. I knew what she meant, and, stepping back a few paces, came running forward and leaped into the air. I cleared the intervening space with no more effort than I could have jumped less than half that distance on earth.

Miela flew over beside me.

"You see, Alan, my husband, it is not so bad, perhaps, that I can fly."

She was smiling whimsically, but I could see her eyes were full of pride.

"There is no other man on Mercury who could do that, Alan," she added.

I tried successive leaps then, always with the same result. I calculated that here the pull of gravity must be something less than one-half that on the earth. It was far more than father had believed.

Miela watched my antics, laughing and clapping her hands with delight. I found I tired very quickly—that is, I was winded. This I attributed to the greater density of the air I was breathing.

In five minutes I was back at Miela's side, panting heavily.

"If I can—ever get so I breathe right—" I said.

She nodded. "A very little time, I think."

I sat down for a moment to recover my breath. Miela explained then that we were some ten miles from the fertile country surrounding the city in which her mother lived, and about fifteen miles from the outskirts of the city itself. I give these distances as they would be measured on earth. We decided to start at once. We took nothing with us. The journey would be a short one, and we could easily return at some future time for what we had left behind. We needed no food for so short a trip, and plenty of water was at hand.

Only one thing Miela would not part with—the single memento she had brought from earth to her mother. She refused to let me touch it, but insisted on carrying it herself, guarding it jealously.

It was Beth's little ivory hand mirror!

We started off. Miela had wound the filmy scarf about her shoulders again with a pretty little gesture.

"I need not use wings, Alan, when I am with you. We shall go together, you and I—on the ground."

And then, as I started off vigorously, she added plaintively from behind me: "If—if you will go slow, my husband, or will wait for me."

I altered my pace to suit hers. I had quite recovered my breath now, and for the moment felt that I could carry her much faster than she could walk. I did gather her into my arms once, and ran forward briskly, while she laughed and struggled with me to be put down. She seemed no more than a little child in my arms; but, as before, the heavy air so oppressed me that in a few moments I was glad enough to set her again upon her feet.

The valley broadened steadily as we advanced. For several miles the look of the ground remained unchanged. I wondered what curious sort of metal this might be—so like copper in appearance. I doubted if it were copper, since even in this hot, moist air it seemed to have no property of oxidation.

I asked Miela about it, and she gave me its Mercutian name at once; but of course that helped me not a bit. She added that outcroppings of it, almost in the pure state, like the great deposits of native copper I had seen on earth, occurred in many parts of Mercury.

I remembered then Bob Trevor's mention of it as the metal of the apparatus used by the invaders of Wyoming.

We went on three or four miles without encountering a single sign of life. No insects stirred underfoot; no birds flew overhead. We might have been—by the look of it—alone on a dead planet.

"Is none of your mountain country inhabited, Miela?" I asked.

She shook her head.

"Only on the plains do people live. There is very little of good land in the Light Country, and so many people. That it is which has caused much trouble in the past. It is for that, many times, the Twilight People have made war upon us."

I found myself constantly able to breathe more easily. Our progress down the valley seemed now irritatingly slow, for I felt I could walk or run three times faster than Miela. Finally I suggested to her that she fly, keeping near me; and that I would make the best speed forward I could. She stared at me quizzically. Then, seeing I was quite sincere, she flung her little arms up about my neck and pulled me down to kiss her.

"Oh, Alan—the very best husband in all the universe, you are. None other could there be—like you."

She had just taken off her scarf again when suddenly I noticed a little speck in the sky ahead. It might have been a tiny bird, flying toward us from the plains below.

"Miela—look!"

She followed the direction of my hand. The speck grew rapidly larger.

"A girl, Alan," she said after a moment. "Let us wait."

We stood silent, watching. It was indeed a girl, flying over the valley some two or three hundred feet above the ground. As she came closer I saw her wings were blue, not red like Miela's. She came directly toward us.

Suddenly Miela gave a little cry.

"Anina! Anina!"

Without a word to me she spread her wings and flew up to meet the oncoming girl.

I stood in awe as I watched them. They met almost above me, and I could see them hovering with clasped hands while they touched cheeks in affectionate greeting. Then, releasing each other, they flew rapidly away together—smaller and smaller, until a turn in the valley hid them entirely from my sight.

I sat down abruptly. A lump was in my throat, a dismal lonesomeness in my heart. I knew Miela would return in a moment—that she had met some friend or relative—yet I could not suppress the vague feeling of sorrow and the knowledge of my own incapacity that swept over me.

For the first time then I wanted wings—wanted them myself—that I might join this wife I loved in her glorious freedom of the air. And I realized, too, for the first time, how that condition Miela so deplored on Mercury had come to pass. I could understand now very easily how it was that married women were deprived by their husbands of these wings which they themselves were denied by the Creator.

Hardly more than ten minutes had passed before I saw the two girls again flying toward me. They alighted a short distance away, and approached me, hand in hand.

The girl with Miela, I could see now, was somewhat shorter, even slighter of build, and two or three years younger. Her face held the same delicate, wistful beauty. The two girls strongly resembled one another in feature. The newcomer was dressed in similar fashion to Miela—sandals on her feet, and silken trousers of a silvery white, fastened at the ankles with golden cords.

Her wings, as I have said, were blue—a delight light blue that, as I afterward noticed, matched her eyes. Her hair was the color of spun gold; she wore it in two long, thick braids over her shoulders and fastened at the waist and knee. She was, in very truth, the most ethereal human being I had ever beheld. And—next to Miela—the most beautiful.

Miela pulled her forward, and she came on, blushing with the sweet shyness of a child. She was winding her silken silver scarf about her breast hastily, as best she could with her free hand.

"My sister, Anina—Alan," said Miela simply.

The girl stood undecided; then, evidently obeying Miela's swift words of instruction, she stood up on tiptoe, put her arms about my neck, and kissed me full on the lips.

Miela laughed gayly.

"You must love her very much, Alan. And she—your little sister—will love you, too. She is very sweet."

Then her face sobered suddenly.

"Tao has returned, Alan. And he has sent messengers to our city. They are appealing to our people to join Tao in his great conquest. They say Tao has here with him, on Mercury, a captive earth -man, with wonderful strength of body, who will help in the destruction of his own world!"

THE CAPTIVE EARTH-MAN

As we came out of the valley I had my first view of the Great City. It occupied a huge, mound-shaped circular mountain which rose alone out of the wide plain that spread before me. As far as I could see extended a rich muddy soil partially covered with water. A road led out of the valley, stretching across these wet fields toward the base of the mountain. It was built on an embankment some eight or ten feet high, of the red, metallic ore of the mountains.

All along the base of this embankment, with their roots in the water, graceful trees like palms curved upward over the road. The landscape was dotted with these and other tropical trees; the scene was, indeed, essentially tropical.

I wondered at the continued absence of sight of human beings. The fields were quite evidently under cultivation. A rise of ground off to the left was ridged with terraces. As we passed on along the road I saw a rude form of plow standing where it had been left in a field which evidently was producing rice or something akin to it. Yet there was not a person in sight. Only ahead in the sky I could see a little cluster of black dots that Miela said was a group of females hovering about the summit of the Great City.

"It is the time of sleep now, Alan," she said, in answer to my question.

I had not thought of that. It was broad daylight, but here on Mercury there was no day or night, but always the same half light, as of a cloudy day.

The mountain on which the city was built was dotted thickly with palms, and as we approached I made out the houses of the city, set amid the trees, with broad streets converging at the top. As we came still closer I saw that the summit of the mountain was laid out like some beautiful tropical garden, with a broad, low-lying palace in its center.

When we were still a mile or so away from the outskirts of the city Miela spoke in her soft native tongue to Anina. The girl smiled at me in parting, and, unwinding the veil from about her breast, flew into the air.

We stood watching her as she winged her way onward toward the sleeping city. When she had dwindled to a tiny speck I sighed unconsciously and turned away; and again Miela smiled at me with comprehension.

We started forward, Miela chattering now like a little child. She seemed eager to tell me all about the new world of hers I was entering, and there was indeed so much to tell she was often at a loss what to describe first.

THE FIRE PEOPLE

She named the cereal which constituted the only crop to which these marsh lands were suitable. From her description I made out it was similar to rice, only of a somewhat larger grain. It formed, she said, the staple article of food of the nation.

As we approached the base of the Great City mountain the ground began gradually rising. The drainage thus afforded made it constantly drier as we advanced. It assumed now more the character of a heavy loam.

Still farther on we began passing occasional houses—the outskirts of the city itself. They were square, single-story, ugly little buildings, built of reddish stone and clay, flat-roofed, and raised a foot or two off the ground on stone pilings. They had large rectangular windows, most of them open, a few with lattice shades. The doorways stood open without sign of a door; access to the ground was obtained by a narrow board incline.

Interspersed with these stone houses I saw many single-room shacks, loosely built of narrow boards from the palm trees, and thatched with straw. In these, Miela explained, lived poorer people, who worked in the rice fields for the small land owners.

We reached the base of the mountain proper, and I found myself in a broad street with houses on both sides. This street seemed to run directly to the summit of the mountain, sloping upward at a sharp angle. We turned into it and began our climb into the sleeping city. It was laid out regularly, all its principal streets running from the base of the mountain upward to its summit, where they converged in a large open space in which the castle I have already mentioned was situated. The cross-streets formed concentric rings about the mountain, at intervals of perhaps five hundred feet down its sides—small circles near the top, lengthening until at the base the distance around was, I should judge, ten miles or more.

We climbed upward nearly to the summit; then Miela turned into one of the cross-streets. I had found the climb tremendously tiring, though Miela seemed not to notice it unduly, and I was glad enough when we reached this street which girdled the mountain almost at the same level. We had gone only a short distance along it, however, when Miela paused before a house set somewhat back from the road on a terrace.

"My home," she said, and her voice trembled a little with emotion. "Our home it shall be now, Alan, with Lua and Anina, our mother and sister."

A low, bushy hedge separated the street from a garden that surrounded the house. The building was of stone, two stories in height. It was covered with a thick vine

66

bearing a profusion of vivid red flowers. On its flat roof were tiny palm trees, a pergola with trellised vines, and still more flowers, most of them of the same brilliant red. The whole was surrounded by a waist -high parapet.

One corner of the roof was covered with thatch—a little nest where one might be sheltered from the rain, and in which I could see a bed of palm fiber. At one side of the house a tremendous cluster of bamboo curved upward and over the roof. A path of chopped coconut husks led from the street to a short flight of steps in the terrace at the front entrance.

We passed along this path and entered through the open doorway directly into what I judged was the living room of the dwelling. It was some thirty feet long and half as broad, with a high ceiling and stone floor. Its three windows fronted the garden we had just left; in its farther wall a low archway led into an adjoining room. The furniture consisted only of two or three small tables and several low, wide couches, all of bamboo.

A woman and the girl Anina rose as we entered. Anina ran toward us eagerly; the elder woman stood, quietly waiting. She was about forty years of age, as tall as Miela, but heavier of build. She was dressed in loose silk trousers, gathered at waist and ankle; and a wide sash that covered her breast. Her hair was iron gray, cut short at the base of the neck. From her shoulders I saw hanging a cloak that entirely covered her wings.

As she turned toward us I saw a serious, dignified, wholly patrician face, with large, kindly dark eyes, a high, intellectual forehead, and a firm yet sensitive mouth. She was the type of woman one would instinctively mark for leader.

Miela ran forward to greet her mother, falling upon her knees and touching her forehead to the elder woman's sandaled feet. As she rose I could see there were tears in the eyes of them both. Then Miela presented me. I stood for an instant, confused, not knowing quite what I should do.

Miela laughed her gay little laugh.

"Bow low, Alan—as I did—to our mother."

I knelt to her respectfully, and she put her hands lightly upon my head, speaking low words of greeting. Then, as I stood up again, I met her eyes and smiled an answer to the gentle smile on her lips. From that moment I felt almost as though she were my own mother, and I am sure she took me then into her heart as her son.

THE FIRE PEOPLE

The introduction over, I turned toward one of the windows, leaving Miela to talk with her mother. Anina followed me, standing timidly by my side, with her big, curious eyes looking up into my face.

"You're a sweet, dear little sister," I said, "and I am going to love you very much."

I put my arm about her shoulders, and she smiled as though she understood me, yielding to my embrace with the ready friendship of a child. For some moments we stood together, looking out of the window and talking to each other with words that were quite unintelligible to us both. Then Miela suddenly called me.

"We shall eat now, Alan," she said, "for you are hungry, I know. And above there is water, that we may wash." Her face clouded as she went on: "Our mother has told me a little that has happened. It is very serious, Alan, as you shall hear. Tao, with his great news of your wonderful world, is very fast winning over our men to his cause. A revolt, there may be, here in our own city—a revolution against our government, our king. We can only look to you now, my husband, to save our country from Tao as well as your own."

The situation as I found it in the Light Country was, as Miela said, alarmingly serious. During the two years Tao had been in the Twilight Country, preparing for his attack upon the earth, his project had caused little stir among the Light Country people.

Its women were, at first, perturbed at this wanton attack upon the humanity of another world, but since the earth was such an unknown quantity, and the fact of its being inhabited at all was problematical, interest in the affair soon lagged. The government of the Light Country concerned itself not at all.

But now, upon Tao's return, the news of his venture, as told by the emissaries he sent to the Light Country, struck its people like a bombshell. These emissaries—all men—had come to the Great City, and, finding their presence tolerated by the authorities, had immediately started haranguing the people.

The men were inclined to listen, and many of them openly declared their sympathy with Tao. These, however, were for the most part of the poorer, more ignorant classes, or those more adventurous, less scrupulous individuals to whom the prospect of sudden riches appealed.

"Why doesn't your government just throw Tao's men out if they're causing so much trouble?" I asked. "They never should have been allowed in the country at all."

Miela smiled sadly. "That is so, my husband. That should have been done; but now it is too late. Our men would protect them now, declaring their right to stay here and speak. There might be bloodshed among our people, and that must not be."

"Are they armed?" I asked.

She shook her head. "No one is armed with the light-ray. To carry it is a crime punishable by death, for the light is too destructive."

"But Tao has it?"

"Tao has it, indeed, but he is not so great a monster that he would use it against us."

I was not so sure of that, and I said so. "You don't mean to tell me, Miela, that your government has allowed Tao to prepare all this destructive armament without itself arming?"

Again she shook her head. "We have been preparing, too, and all our young men can be called if occasion comes. But that must never be. It would be too terrible."

Miela and I occupied, that first night on Mercury, a broad wooden bed built low to the floor, with a mattress of palm fiber. At first I could not sleep, but lay thinking over the many things she had told me. The light in the room, too, was strange. Lattice covered the windows, but it was like trying to sleep at midday; and the heat and heaviness of the air oppressed me. I dropped off finally, to be awakened by Miela's voice calling me to breakfast.

We sat down to the morning meal at a low table set with shining plates and goblets of copper, or whatever the metal was, and napery of silk. The rice formed our main article of food, with sugar, milk, and a beverage not unlike coffee. There was also a meat like beef, although more highly flavored, and a number of sickish sweet fruits of a kind entirely new to me, which I could do no more than taste.

We were served by a little maid whose darker skin and heavier features proclaimed her of another race—a native of the Fire Country, Miela told me. She was dressed in a brown tunic of heavy silk, reaching from waist to knee. Her thick black hair was cut to her shoulders.

On her left arm above the elbow was welded a broad band of copper inscribed with a mark to identify Lua as her owner, for she was a slave. Her torso was bare, except for a cloak like Lua's which hung from her shoulders in the back to cover her wings. By this I knew she could not fly.

THE FIRE PEOPLE

It was not until some time afterward that I learned the reason for this covering of the clipped wings. The wing joints were severed just above the waist line. The feathers on the remaining upper portions were clipped, but through disuse these feathers gradually dropped out entirely.

The flesh and muscle underneath was repulsive in appearance—for which reason it was always kept covered. Lua showed me her wings once—mere shrunken stumps of what had once been her most glorious possession. I did not wonder then that the women were ready to fight, almost, rather than part with them.

Difficulties of language made our conversation during the meal somewhat halting, although Miela acted as interpreter. Lua and Anina both expressed their immediate determination to learn English, and, with the same persistence that Miela had shown, they set aside nearly everything else to accomplish it.

We decided that we should see the king and arrange our future course of action. Whatever was to be done should be done at once—that we all agreed—for Tao's men were steadily gaining favor with a portion of the people, and we had no means of knowing what they would attempt to do.

"What will your people think of me?" I suddenly asked Miela.

"We have sent our king word that you are here," she answered, "and we have asked that he send a guard to take you to the castle this morning."

"A guard?"

She smiled. "It is better that the people see you first as a man of importance. You will go to the king under guard. Few will notice you. Then will he, our ruler, arrange that you are shown to the people as a great man—one who has come here to help us—one who is trusted and respected by our king. You see, my husband, the difference?"

I did, indeed, though I wondered a little how I should justify this exalted position which was being thrust upon me. After breakfast Lua and Anina busied themselves about the house, while Miela and I went to the rooftop to wait for the king's summons. From here I had my first really good view of the city at close range.

Miela's home sat upon a terrace, leveled off on the steep hillside; all the houses in the vicinity were similarly situated. Behind us the mountain rose steeply; in front it dropped away, affording an extended view of the level, palm-dotted country below.

The slope of hillside rising abruptly behind us held another house just above the level of the rooftop we were on. As I sat there looking idly about I thought I saw a

70

figure lurking near this higher building. I called Miela's attention to it—the obscure figure of a man standing against a huge palm trunk.

As we watched the figure stepped into plainer view. I saw then it was a man, evidently looking down at us. I stood up. There was no one else in sight except a woman on the roof of the other house holding an infant.

Something about the man's figure seemed vaguely familiar; my heart leaped suddenly.

"Miela," I whispered, "surely that—that is no one of your world."

Her hand clutched my arm tightly as the man stepped forward again and waved at us. I crossed the rooftop, Miela following. At my sudden motion the man hesitated, then seemed about to run. I hardly know what thoughts impelled me, but suddenly I shouted: "Wait!"

At the sound of my voice he whirled around, stopped dead an instant, and then, with an answering call, came running down the hillside.

"The earth -man!" cried Miela. "The earth -man of Tao it must be."

We hurried down through the house and arrived at its back entrance. Coming toward us at a run across the garden was the man—unmistakably one of my own world.

My hurried glance showed me he was younger than I—a short, stocky, red -headed chap, dressed in dirty white duck trousers and a torn white linen shirt.

He came on at full speed.

"Hello!" I called.

He stopped abruptly. For an instant we stared at each other; then he grinned broadly.

"Well, I don't know who you are," he ejaculated, "but I want to say it certainly does me good to see you."

THE RULER OF THE LIGHT COUNTRY

However pleased the newcomer was to see me, I had no difficulty in assuring him with equal truth that my feelings matched his. The first surprise of the meeting over, we took him to the living room, where Lua greeted him with dignified courtesy, and we all gathered around to hear his story.

He was, I saw now, not more than twenty years old, rather short—perhaps five feet six or seven inches—and powerfully built, with a shock of tousled red hair and a handsome, rough -hewn face essentially masculine.

He seemed to be an extraordinarily good -humored chap, with the ready wit of an Irishman. I liked him at once—I think we all did.

He began, characteristically, near the end rather than the beginning of the events I knew he must have to tell us.

"I got away," he chuckled, grinning more broadly than ever. "But where I was going to, search me. And who the deuce are you, if you don't mind my asking? How did you ever get to this God -forsaken place?"

I smiled. "You tell us about yourself first; then I'll tell you about myself. You are the earth -man we've been hearing about, aren't you—the man Tao captured in Wyoming and brought here with him?"

"They caught me in Wyoming all right. Who's Tao?"

"He's the leader of them all."

"Oh. Well, they brought me here, as you say, and I guess they've had me about all over this little earth since. They stuck me in a boat, and Lord knows how far we went. We got here last night, and when my guard went to sleep I beat it." He scratched his head lugubriously. "Though what good I thought it was going to do me I don't know. That's about all, I guess. Who the deuce are you?"

I laughed.

"Wait a minute—don't go so fast. Start at the beginning. What's your name?"

"Oliver Mercer."

His face grew suddenly grave. "My brother was killed up there in Wyoming—that's how I happened to go there in the first place."

"Mercer!" I exclaimed.

He started. "Yes—why? You don't think you know me, by any chance, do you?"

"No, but I knew your brother—that is, I know Bob Trevor, who was with him when he was killed. He's one of my best friends."

72

The young fellow extended his hand. "A friend of Bob Trevor's—away off here! Don't it get you, just?"

Miela interrupted us here to translate to her mother and Anina what he said.

Mercer went on: "The assumption is, you people here are not working with this gang of crooks I got away from—this Tao? Am I right in thinking so?"

"You're certainly right, that far," I laughed.

I felt, more than I can say, a great sense of relief, a lessening of the tension, the unconscious strain I had been under, at this swift, jovial conversation with another human of my own kind.

"Yes, you're right on that. This Tao and I are not exactly on the same side. I'll tell you all about it in a minute."

"Then, we're working together?"

"Yes."

"Well, all I'm working for is to get back home where I came from."

"You won't be when you hear all I've got to say."

He started at that; then, with sudden change of thought, his eyes turned to Anina. The girl blushed under his admiring gaze.

"Say, she's a little beauty, isn't she? Who is she?"

"She's my sister," I said, smiling.

For once he was too dumfounded to reply.

Miela had finished her translation now, and, as she turned back to us, spoke in English for the first time during the conversation.

"Do you know why it is they brought you here from the Twilight Country?" she asked Mercer.

This gave him another shock. "Why, I—no. That is—say, how do you happen to talk English? Is it one of your languages here, by any chance?"

Miela laughed gayly.

"Only we three, in all this world, speak English. I know it because—"

I interrupted her.

"Suppose I tell him our whole story, Miela? Then—"

"That's certainly what I want to hear," said Mercer emphatically. "And especially why it is that I'm not supposed to want to get back to where I belong."

My explanation must have lasted nearly an hour, punctuated by many questions and exclamations of wonder from young Mercer. I told him the whole affair in detail, and ended with a statement of exactly how matters stood now on Mercury.

THE FIRE PEOPLE

"Do you want to hurry back home to earth now?" I finished.

"Duck out of this? I should say not. Why, we've got a million things to do here." His eyes turned again toward Anina.

"And, say—about letting those girls keep their wings. I'm strong for that. Let's be sure and fix that up before we leave."

It was not more than half an hour later when the king's guards arrived to conduct us to the castle. Meanwhile young Mercer had discovered he was hungry and thirsty. As soon as he had finished eating we started off—he and I, with Lua and Miela. The guards led us away as though we were prisoners, forming a hollow square—there were some thirty of them—with us in the center. We attracted little attention from passersby; the few who stopped to stare at us, or who attempted to follow, were briskly ordered away.

Occasionally a few girls would hover overhead, but when the guards shouted up at them they flew away obediently.

The king's castle was constructed of metal and stone—a long, low, rambling structure, flanked by two spires or minarets, giving it somewhat an Oriental appearance. Each of these minarets was girdled, halfway up, by a narrow balcony.

The first room into which we passed was small, seemingly an antechamber. From it, announced by two other guards who stood at the entrance, we entered directly into the main hall of the building. At one end of it there was a raised platform. On this, seated about a large table, were some ten or twelve dignitaries—the king's advisers. They were, I saw, all aged men, with beardless, seamed faces, long snowy -white hair to their shoulders, and dressed in flowing silk robes.

The king was a man of seventy -odd, kindly faced, gentle in demeanor. He bore himself with the dignity of a born ruler, and yet his very kindliness of aspect and the doddering gravity of his aged councilors, seemed to explain at once most of the trouble that now confronted him.

We stood beside this table—they courteously made way for Lua to sit among them—and all its occupants immediately turned to face us.

Our audience lasted perhaps an hour and a half altogether. I need not go into details. I was right in assuming that the king desired to help us prevent Tao from his attempted conquest of the earth. This was so, but only in so far as his actions would not jeopardize the peace of his own nation. He sadly admitted his error in allowing Tao's emissaries into the Light Country. But now they were there, he did not see how to get them out.

His people were daily listening to them more eagerly; and, what was worse, the police guards themselves seemed rather more in sympathy with them than otherwise. A slight disturbance had occurred in the streets the day before, and the guards had stood apathetically by, taking no part. Above all else, the king stoutly protested, he would have no bloodshed in his country if he could prevent it.

In the neighboring towns of the Light Country—the nearest of which was some forty miles away from the Great City—the situation was almost the same. Reports brought by young women flying between the cities said that to many Tao also had sent emissaries who were fast winning converts to his cause.

"Do all these people who believe in Tao expect to go to our earth when it is conquered?" I asked Miela. "How can they—so many of them—hope to benefit in that way? Aren't they satisfied here?"

Miela smiled sadly.

"No people can ever be satisfied—all of them. That you must know, my husband. They have many grievances against our ruler. Many things they want which he cannot give. Tao may promise these things—and if they believe his promise it is very bad."

"He might come over here and try to make himself king," Mercer said suddenly. "If it's like that maybe he could do it, too, with this grand earth -conquest getting ready. Tell the king that—see what he says."

"He says that he realizes and fears it," Miela answered. "But he thinks that first Tao will go to your earth, and he may never come back. So much may happen—"

"So he's just going to wait," I explained. "Well, we're not just going to wait. Ask the king what our status is."

"Ask him about me," Mercer put in. "Are those Tao men going to grab me the minute I show my face on the street, or will he protect me?"

Miela translated this to the king, adding something of her own to which he evidently agreed.

"It is as I thought," she said. "He believes he can present you to the people as men of earth who are our guests, and that they will accept you in friendly spirit, most of them."

The king spoke to one of his advisers, who abruptly left the room.

"He will call the people now," Miela went on, "and will speak to them from the tower—all who can leave their tasks to come. You will stand there with him. He will ask that we of the Light Country allow you to remain here in peace among us. And this captive earth man of Tao's"—she laid her hand lightly on Mercer's shoulder—"he will ask, too, that he be given sanctuary among us. Our people still are kindly—most of them—and they will see the justice of what he asks."

I suggested then that Miela tell the king that we had determined, if we could, to frustrate Tao in his plans; and showed her how to point out to him that such an outcome would, if successful, make his throne secure and insure peace for his nation.

He asked me bluntly what it was I thought I could do. The vague beginnings of a plan were forming in my mind. "Tell him, Miela, I think we can rid the Light Country of Tao's emissaries—send them back—without causing any disturbances among the people. Ask him if that would not be a good thing."

The king nodded gravely as this was translated.

"He asks you how?" Miela said next.

"Tell him, Miela, that there are some things that might happen of which he would be very glad, but which it might be better he did not know. You understand. Make him see that we will be responsible for this—that he needn't have anything to do with it or know anything about it. Then, if we do anything wrong against your laws, he will be perfectly safe in stopping and punishing us."

Miela nodded, and began swiftly telling this to the king. As she spoke I saw his eyes twinkle and a swift little series of nods from the aged men about the table made me know that I had carried my point. During the latter part of this talk I had noticed the growing murmur of voices outside the castle. The old man who had left the room at the king's order came back.

"The people now are gathering," Miela said. "In a moment we shall go up into the tower."

The king's councilors now rose and withdrew, and a few moments later the king, without formality, led the four of us through the castle and up into the tower.

We climbed a little stone staircase in the tower and came into a circular room some sixty feet above the ground. A small doorway from this room gave access to the narrow balcony which girdled the tower. The sounds of the gathering crowd came up plainly from the gardens below. We waited for a time, and then, at a sign from the king, stepped together upon the balcony.

The gardens below were full of people—gathered among the palms and moving about for points of vantage from which to obtain a view of the balcony. Most of them were men and older women. The girls were, nearly all of them, in the air, flying about the tower and hovering near the balcony, staring at us curiously. The women were, for the most part, dressed as I have described Lua.

The men wore knee -length trousers of fabric or leather, and sometimes a shirt or leather jacket, although a difference of costume that made evident the rank of the wearer was noticeable in both sexes. All were bareheaded, with the exception of the king's guards, who were thus plainly distinguishable, standing idly about among the crowd.

As we stepped out into view of the people a louder murmur arose, mingled with a ripple of applause. Three or four girls, hovering only a few feet in front of us, clapped their hands and laughed. The king placed Mercer and me on either side of him, and, standing with his hands on our shoulders, leaned over the balcony rail and began to speak.

A silence fell over the crowd; they listened quietly, but with none of that respect and awe with which a people usually faces its king.

Miela whispered to me. "He is telling them about your earth, and that you came here to visit us in friendly spirit."

There were some murmurs of dissent as the king proceeded, and once some bolder individual shouted up a question, at which a wave of laughter arose. As it died away, and the crowd appeared to listen to the king's next words, a stone suddenly came whirling up from below, narrowly missing the king's head. A sudden hush fell over the people at this hostile act; then a tumult of shouting broke loose, and a commotion off to one side showed where the offender was standing.

Mercer wheeled toward me, his face white with anger.

"Who did that—did you see him ? Which one was it?"

The king began to speak, as if nothing had occurred, and an instant later several more stones whistled past us. The commotion in the crowd grew more violent, but it was evident that a great majority of the people were against this demonstration.

"It is better we go inside," Miela said quietly.

The king was shouting down to his guards now, but they stood apathetically by, taking no part.

Another stone hurtled past us, striking the tower and falling at our feet. The king abruptly ceased his shouting and left the balcony. As he passed me and I glanced into his frightened face I felt a sudden sense of pity for this gentle, kindly old man, so well -meaning, but so utterly ineffective as a ruler.

THE FIRE PEOPLE

I was about to pull Miela back into the room when a girl flew up to the balcony railing. As she balanced herself upon it I saw it was Anina. She said something to Miela, who turned swiftly to me.

"She is right, my husband. We must not leave the matter like this. They can have no confidence in you—our women most of all—if you do not do something now. A sign of your strength now would make them respect you—perhaps one of those who threw the stones you could punish."

I knew she was right. Most of the crowd was with us. If we retreated now, those against us would grow bolder—our appearance on the street might at any time be dangerous. But if now we proved ourselves superior in strength, the popular sentiment in our favor would be just that much stronger. At least, that is the way it seemed to me.

I did not need to ask Mercer's opinion, for at Miela's words he immediately said: "That's my idea. Just give me a chance at them."

He leaned over the balcony. "How are we going to get down there? It's too far to drop."

Miela spoke to Anina, and they both flew away. In a moment they were back with two other girls. All four clung to the outside of the balcony railing, and formed a cross with their joined hands. Into this little seat of their arms I clambered. My weight was too great for them to have lifted me up, but they fluttered safely with me to the ground, landing in a heap among the people, who had cleared a space to receive us. As soon as I was upon my feet the girls flew back for Mercer, and in a moment more he was beside me.

"If we only knew who threw those stones," I said.

I stood erect, and my greater height enabled me to see over the heads of the people easily.

Miela laid her hand on my arm.

"One of them I know. His name is Baar, a bad character. He has caused much trouble in the past."

She then told me hastily that she and Anina would fly up and seek him out. Mercer and I were to follow them through the crowd on the ground.

The throng was pushing close about us now, although those nearest us tried to keep away as best they could. Miela and Anina flew up over our heads, and, side by side, Mercer and I started off. The people struggled back before our advance, striving to make a path for us. At times the press of those behind made it impossible for them to give us room. We did not hesitate, but shoved our way forward, elbowing them away roughly.

Suddenly, some twenty feet ahead of us, I saw Miela and Anina come to the ground, and in a moment more we were with them again.

The crowd was less dense here, and about us there was a considerable open space, Miela pointed out a man leaning against the trunk of a palm tree near by and glaring at us malevolently.

"That is he," she said quietly. "A very bad man—this Baar—whom many would like to see punished."

Mercer jumped forward, but I swept him back with my arm.

"Leave him to me," I said. "You stand here by the girls. If I need you, I'll shout."

The man by the tree was a squat little individual, some five feet three or four inches tall, and extraordinarily broad. He was bareheaded, with black hair falling to his shoulders. He was naked to the waist, exposing a powerful torso. His single garment was the usual knee -length trousers. I thought I had never seen so evil a face as his, as he stood there, holding his ground before my slow advance, and leering at me. His cheek bones were high, his jowls heavy, his little eyes set wide apart. His nose was flat, as though it had once been broken.

I went straight up to him, and he did not move. There were certainly three hundred people watching us as I stood there facing him.

"You threw a stone at your king," I said to him sternly, although I knew perfectly well he could not understand my words. "You shall be punished."

I reached out suddenly and struck him in the face as smartly as I could with the flat of my hand. He gave a roar of surprise and pain, and as soon as he could recover from my blow lunged at me with a snarl of rage.

As he came I turned and darted swiftly away. I heard a shout of surprise from Mercer. "It's all right," he called. "Wait."

I ran about twenty feet, then turned and waited. The man came on, head down, charging like a mad bull. When he was close upon me I gathered my muscles and sprang clear over his head, landing well behind him.

He stopped and looked around confusedly, evidently not quite sure at first what had become of me.

Mercer gave a shout of glee, and, to my great satisfaction, I heard it taken up by the crowd, mingled with murmurs of surprise and awe.

THE FIRE PEOPLE

I stood quiet, and again my opponent charged me. I eluded him easily, and then for fully ten minutes I taunted and baited him this way, as a skillful toreador taunts his bull. The crowd now seemed to enjoy the affair hugely.

Finally I darted behind my adversary and, catching him by the shoulders, tripped him and laid him on his back on the ground A great roar of laughter went up from the onlookers.

The man was on his feet again in an instant, breathing heavily, for indeed he had nearly winded himself by his exertions. I ran over to Mercer.

"Go on," I said; "show them what you can do."

The commotion of this contest had drawn many other spectators about us now, but they kept a space clear, pushing back hurriedly before our sudden rushes. At my words Mercer darted forward eagerly. His first move was to leap some twenty feet across the open space. This smaller opponent seemed to give the Mercutian new courage.

He shouted exultantly and dashed at Mercer, who stood quietly waiting for him at the edge of the crowd.

Mercer's ideas evidently were different from mine, for as his adversary came within reach he stepped nimbly aside and hit him a vicious blow in the face. The man toppled over backward and lay still.

I ran over to where Mercer was bending over his fallen foe. As I came up he straightened and grinned at me. "Oh, shucks," he said disgustedly. "You can't fight up here—it's too easy."

THE MOUNTAIN CONCLAVE

"It is reasonable," Miela said thoughtfully. "And that our women will help as you say—of that I am sure."

We were gathered in the living room after the evening meal, and I had given them my ideas of how we should start meeting the situation that confronted us. We had had no more trouble that day. After the encounter in the king's garden Mercer and I had followed the two girls swiftly home. We were not molested in the streets, although the people crowded about us wherever we went.

"Why did none of Baar's friends come to his rescue up there in the garden?" I asked Miela. "Surely there must have been many of them about."

"They were afraid, perhaps," she answered. "And they knew the people were against them. There might have been serious trouble; for that is not their way—to fight in the open."

Her face became very grave. "We must be very careful, my husband, that they, or Tao's men do not come here to harm you while you sleep."

"Why do you suppose they ever happened to bring me here in the first place?" Mercer wanted to know. "That's what I can't figure out."

"They knew not that Alan was here," said Miela. "I think they wanted to show you to our people as their captive—one of the earth-men."

Mercer chuckled.

"They didn't know what a good runner I was, or they'd never have taken a chance like that."

I told Miela then my plan for enlisting the sympathy of the women of the Light Country and for securing the active coöperation of the girls in ridding us of the disturbing presence of these Tao emissaries.

We planned that whatever we did should be in secret, so far as possible. Mercer and I talked together, while Miela consulted with Lua at length.

I explained to Mercer that Tao might at any time send an expedition to invade the Light Country.

"How about that car we came from earth in?" he suggested. "He could sail over in that, couldn't he—if he should want to come over here?"

I knew that was not feasible. In the outer realms of space the balancing attractions of the different heavenly bodies made it easy enough to head in any specified direction; but for travel over a planet's surface it was quite impractical. Its rise and fall could be perfectly governed; but when it was directed laterally the case was very different. Just where it would go could not be determined with enough exactness.

Miela turned back to us from her consultation with Lua.

"In the mountains, high up and far beyond the Valley of the Sun," she said, "lies a secret place known only to our women. Our mother says that she and I and Anina can spread the news among our virgins to gather there to -morrow at the time of sleep. Only to those we know we can trust will we speak—and they will have no men to whom to tell our plans. To -morrow they will gather up there in the clouds, among the crags, unseen by prying eyes. And you and our—our friend Ollie"—she smiled as she used the nickname by which he had asked her to call him—"you two we will take there by the method you have told us. We will arrange, up there in secret, what it is we are to do to help our world and yours."

This, in effect, was our immediate plan of procedure. Nearly all the next day Mercer and I stayed about the house, while the three women went through the city quietly, calling forth all those they could reach to our conclave in the mountains.

They returned some time after midday. Miela came first, alighting with a swift, triumphant swoop upon the roof where Mercer and I were sitting.

One glance at her face told me she had been successful.

"They will come, my husband," she announced. "And they are ready and eager, all of them, to do what they can."

Anina and Lua brought the same news. When we were all together again Mercer and I took them to the garden behind the house and showed them what we had done while they were away.

It was my plan to have the girls carry Mercer and me through the air with them. For that purpose we had built a platform of bamboo, which now lay ready in the garden.

Miela clapped her hands at sight of it. "That is perfect, my husband. No difficulty will there be in taking you with us now."

The platform was six feet wide by ten long. It rested upon a frame with two poles of bamboo some forty feet in length running lengthwise along its edges. These two poles thus projected in front and back of the platform fifteen feet each way. Running under them crosswise at intervals were other, shorter bamboo lengths which projected out the sides a few feet to form handles. There were ten of them on a side at intervals of four feet.

I found it difficult to realize the difference between night and day, since here on Mercury the light never changed. I longed now for that darkness of our own earth which would make it so much easier for us to conceal our movements. Miela relieved my mind on that score, however, by explaining that at nearly the same hour almost every one in the city fell asleep. The physical desire for sleep was, I learned, much stronger with the Mercutians than with us; and only by the drinking of a certain medicinal beverage could they ward it off.

It was after the evening meal, at a time which might have corresponded to an hour or so before midnight, that the selected eighteen girls began to arrive. Miela brought them into the living room with us until they were all together.

It was a curious gathering—this bevy of Mercutian maidens. They all seemed between the ages of sixteen and twenty -three—fragile, dainty little wisps of femininity, yet having a strength in their highly developed wing muscles that was truly surprising.

They were dressed in the characteristic costume I have described, with only a slight divergence of color or ornamentation. They were of only two types—jet black tresses, black eyes, and red -feathered wings like Miela; or the less vivid, more ethereal Anina—blue -eyed, golden -haired, with wing feathers of light blue.

When they had all arrived we went into the garden behind the house. In a moment more Mercer and I were seated side by side on the little bamboo platform. Miela and Anina took the center positions so that they would be near us. The other girls ranged themselves along the sides, each grasping one of the handles.

In another moment we were in the air. My first sensation was one of a sudden rushing forward and upward. The frail little craft swayed under me alarmingly, but I soon grew used to that. The flapping of those many pairs of huge wings so close was very loud; the wind of our swift forward flight whistled past my ears. Looking down over the side of the platform, between the bodies of two of the girls, I could see the city silently dropping away beneath us. Above there was nothing but the same dead gray sky, black in front, with occasional vivid lightning flashes and the rumble of distant thunder.

Underneath the storm cloud, far ahead, the jagged tops of a range of mountains projected above the horizon. As I watched they seemed slowly creeping up and forward as the horizon rolled back to meet them.

For half an hour or so we sped onward through the air. We were over the mountains now. Great jagged, naked peaks of shining metal towered above us, with that broken, utterly desolate country beneath. We swept continually upward, for the mountains rose steadily in broad serrated ranks before us.

Occasionally we would speed up a narrow defile, with the broken, tumbling cliffs rising abruptly over our heads, only to come out above a level plateau or across a cañon a thousand feet deep or more.

The storm broke upon us. We entered a cloud that wrapped us in its wet mist and hid the mountains from our sight. The darkness of twilight settled down, lighted by flashes of lightning darting almost over our heads. The sharp cracks of thunder so close threatened to split my eardrums.

The wind increased in violence. The little platform trembled and swayed. I could see the girls struggling to hold it firm. At times we would drop abruptly straight down a hundred or two hundred feet, with a great fluttering of wings; but all the time I knew we were rising sharply.

Mercer and I clung tightly to the platform. We did not speak, and I think both of us were frightened. Certainly we were awed by the experience. After a time—I have no idea how long—we passed through the storm and came again into the open air with the same gray sky above us.

We were several thousand feet up now, flying over what seemed to be a tumbling mass of small volcanic craters. In front of us rose a sheer cliff wall, extending to the right and left to the horizon. We passed over its rim, and I saw that it curved slightly inward, forming the circumference of a huge circle.

The inner floor was hardly more than a thousand feet down, and seemed fairly level. We continued on, arriving finally over the mouth of a little circular pit. This formed an inner valley, half a mile across and with sheer side walls some five hundred feet high. As we swung down into it I noticed above the horizon behind us a number of tiny black dots in the sky—other girls flying out from the city to our meeting.

I have never beheld so wild, so completely desolate a scene. The ground here was that same shining mass of virgin metal, tumbled about and broken up in hopeless confusion.

Great rugged bowlders lay strewn about; tiny caverns yawned; fissures opened up their unknown depths; sharp -pointed crags reared their heads like spires left standing amid the ruins of some huge cathedral. There was, indeed, hardly a level spot of ground in sight.

I wondered with vague alarm where we should land, for nowhere could I see sufficient space, even for our small platform. We were following closely the line of cliff wall when suddenly we swooped sharply downward and to the right with incredible speed. My heart leaped when, for an instant, I thought something had gone wrong. Then the forward end of the platform tilted abruptly upward; there was a sudden, momentary fluttering of wings, a scrambling as the girls' feet touched the ground, and we settled back and came to rest with hardly more than a slight jar.

Miela stood up, rubbing her arms, which must have ached from her efforts.

"We are here, Alan—safely, as we planned."

We had landed on a little rocky niche that seemed to be in front of the opening of a small cave mouth in the precipitous cliffside. I stood up unsteadily, for I was cramped and stiff, and the solid earth seemed swaying beneath me. I was standing on what was hardly more that a narrow shelf, not over fifteen feet wide and some thirty feet above the base of the cliff.

Mercer was beside me, looking about him with obvious awe.

"What a place!" he ejaculated.

We stepped cautiously to the brink of the ledge and peered over. Underneath us, with the vertical wall of the cliff running directly down into it, spread a small pool of some heavy, viscous fluid, inky black, and with iridescent colors floating upon its surface. It bubbled and boiled lazily, and we could feel its heat on our faces plainly.

Beyond the pool, not more than a hundred yards across, lay a mass of ragged bowlders piled together in inextricable confusion; beyond these a chasm with steam rising from it, whose bottom I could not see—a crack as though the ground had suddenly cooled and split apart. Across the entire surface of this little cliff-bound circular valley it was the same, as though here a tortured nature had undergone some terrible agony in the birth of this world.

The scene, which indeed had something infernal about it, would have been extraordinary enough by itself; but what made it even more so was the fact that several hundred girls were perched among these crags, sitting idle, or standing up and flapping their wings like giant birds, and more were momentarily swooping in from above. I had, for an instant, the feeling that I was Dante, surveying the lower regions, and that here was a host of angels from heaven invading them.

During the next hour fully a thousand girls arrived. There were perhaps fifteen hundred altogether, and only a few stragglers were hastily flying in when we decided to wait no longer.

THE FIRE PEOPLE

Miela flew out around the little valley, calling them to come closer. They came flying toward us and crowded upon the nearer crags just beyond the pool, clutching the precipitous sides, and scrambling for a foothold wherever they could. A hundred or more found place on the ledge with us, or above or below it wherever a slight footing could be found on the wall of the cliff.

When they were all settled, and the scrambling and flapping of wings had ceased, Miela stood up and addressed them. A solemn, almost sinister hush lay over the valley, and her voice carried far. She spoke hardly above the ordinary tone, earnestly, and occasionally with considerable emphasis, as though to drive home some important point.

For nearly half an hour she spoke without a break, then she called me to her side and put one of her wings caressingly about my shoulders. I did not know what she said, but a great wave of handclapping and flapping of wings answered her. She turned to me with glowing face.

"I have told them about your wonderful earth, and Tao's evil plans; and just now I said that you were my husband—and I, a wife, can still fly as well as they. That is a very wonderful thing, Alan. No woman ever, in this world, has been so blessed as I. They realize that—and they respect me and love you for it."

She did not wait for me to speak, but again addressed the assembled girls. When she paused a chorus of shouts answered her. Many of the girls in their enthusiasm lost their uncertain footholds and fluttered about, seeking others. For a moment there was confusion.

"I have told them briefly what we are to do," Miela explained. "First, to rid the Great City of Tao's men, sending them back to the Twilight Country; and do this in all our other cities where they are making trouble. Then, when our nation is free from this danger, we will plan how to deal with Tao direct, for he must not again go to your earth.

"And when all that is done I have said you will do your best to make our men believe as you do, so that never again will our women marry only to lose all that makes their virginity so glorious."

THE FIRE PLANET

I think I should explain now a little about the physical conformation of Mercury—the "lay of the land," so to speak—in order that the events I am about to describe may be more readily understood. It has already been made clear by Bob Trevor, I believe, that Mercury revolves on its axis only once during the time of its revolution around the sun. Thus, just as a similar condition always makes our moon present very nearly the same face to us, so Mercury presents always the same portion of its surface to the sun.

It will be understood, therefore, that, theoretically, there must be on Mercury but one spot where the sun always is directly overhead. It could not be seen, however, owing to the dense clouds. This spot approximates the center of the region known as the Fire Country.

So far as I could learn, it was here that human life on the planet began. Certainly it was the first region where civilization reached any height. When Columbus was discovering America great cities flourished in the Fire Country—cities of untold wealth and beauty, now fallen into ruins like the great cities of our own Aztec and Inca civilizations.

The Fire Country was then like the equatorial regions of earth—a dense, tropic jungle, hotter than most temperatures we have to bear, but still, by reason of its thick enveloping atmosphere of clouds, capable of supporting life in comparative comfort. Its inhabitants were dark-skinned, but rather more like our Indians than Negroid races.

Then, several centuries ago—the exact time is uncertain, for no written records are kept on Mercury—came the Great Storms. Their cause was unknown—some widespread atmospheric disturbance. These storms temporarily parted the clouds in many places, allowing the direct rays of the sun to fall upon the planet's surface. The resulting temperature destroyed all life, withered all vegetation, with its scorching blast. The inhabitants of the Fire Country were killed by hundreds of thousands, their cities deserted, their land laid a desert waste.

These storms, which it appears began suddenly, have returned periodically ever since, making the region practically uninhabitable. Its surviving races, pushed outward toward the more temperate zone, were living, at this time I am describing, in a much lower state of civilization than the people of the Light Country—a civilization of comparative savagery. In the Light Country they were held as slaves.

THE FIRE PEOPLE

This region—thus very aptly known as the Fire Country—embraces a circular area directly underneath the sun. So far as I could learn, it extended outward roughly to those points where—if it had been visible—the sun would have appeared some halfway between zenith and horizon.

Lying outside the circle, in a larger, concentric ring, is the zone known as the Light Country. Entirely free from the equatorial storms, no direct rays of sunlight have ever penetrated its protecting cloud blanket. Here exists the highest state of civilization on the planet.

Beyond the Light Country, in another concentric ring, lies the Twilight Country. It forms a belt about the planet, beginning roughly at those points at which the sun would appear only a short distance above the horizon, and extending back to where the sun would be below the horizon. In this region, as its name implies, there is never more than twilight. It is lightest at the borders of the Light Country, and fades into night at its other side.

Still farther, beyond the twilight zone, lies the region of perpetual night and cold—the Dark Country. This area embraces the rest of the planet, comprising something less than half of its entire surface. Here is eternal night—a night of Stygian darkness, unlighted even by the stars, since the same atmosphere makes them invisible.

The Dark Country, so far as it has been explored—which is very little—is a rocky waste and a sea of solid ice that never melts. Near the borders of the Twilight Country a few people like our Eskimos exist—savages with huge white faces, and great, staring eyes. There are a few fur-bearing animals and birds, but except for this fringe of life the Dark Country is thought to be uninhabited, its terrible cold making life in any form impossible.

So much, in general, for the main geographical features of Mercury. The Great City stands about halfway between the borders of the Fire Country and the edge of the twilight zone. This level marshland, the barren, metallic mountains, and a sort of semitropic jungle, partly inundated by water, comprise nearly all the area of the Light Country.

From the Great City, through the watery jungle, extends a system of little winding bayous—a perfect maze of them, with hundreds of intercommunicating branches—which it would be almost impossible to traverse without losing all sense of direction.

Beyond these bayous, into which their sluggish currents flow, lies the Narrow Sea. On its farther shore begins the Twilight Country, much of it a barren, semifrigid waste, with a little level, tillable land, vast rocky mountain ranges, and a few forests.

In spite of its inhospitable character the Twilight Country is fairly densely populated; and, I realized when I got into it, civilized life is exceedingly difficult to maintain there. I understood then why the Twilight People were so envious of land in the Light Country; and, in truth, I could not blame them for that, or for looking toward our earth with longing.

But just as the Light Country People had defended their borders with implacable determination, so was I determined that they should not invade my world, either. And I was ready to stake my life and even the lives of those I loved here on Mercury in the attempt to prevent them.

THE FIGHT AT THE BAYOU

Miela proceeded to explain our plan in detail to these fifteen hundred enthusiastic allies. It was my idea to build several platforms similar to this one on which Mercer and I had been carried up here into the mountains, only somewhat larger. We then proposed to seize these emissaries of Tao—there were not more than eight or ten of them altogether in the Great City—capturing them at night, without alarm, if possible, and transporting them summarily into the Twilight Country. My theory was that if they were to disappear thus mysteriously the people of the Great City would have no particular cause to make trouble afterward, and we hoped that the affair would soon be forgotten.

Miela thought it practical for us to carry them in this way across the Narrow Sea. The Lone City, from which Tao was operating, was located near the edge of the sea, and if we gave them food they would be enabled to reach it in safety in a day or two. The girls agreed enthusiastically with this plan, and we selected a number to carry it out.

Meanwhile we planned also to organize a system of aärial patrols, and detailed some two hundred of the girls, who in varying shifts were to fly back and forth along the borders of the sea over its Light Country shore, to make sure that Tao did not attempt to make a crossing by water.

"Can't they fly over as well as we can?" Mercer objected. "Their women fly, too, don't they?"

The women of the Twilight Country did fly, but for two reasons we did not fear an attack from them in the air. First, Miela doubted that the women would concern themselves in the affair; they were stupid and apathetic—fit only for child -bearing. The men might, of course, force them to the attempt, but even in that event, Miela explained, it would result in little; for generations of comparative inactivity and the colder climate had made them inclined to stoutness. Their wing muscles were weak and flabby, and with their greater weight of body they flew very badly.

"Suppose Tao should come over?" I suggested to Miela. "I don't believe he will—but if he should, how could we stop him?"

"By water he would come," she answered. "In boats—small they are, I think, those he has. We could not stop him, for the light -ray he would bring. But our women, flying over the ocean, would see him coming, and tell our king. More we could not do now."

"You mean this patrol would give the government the warning it won't obtain for itself? There would be war then? The people would arm to resist invasion?"

Miela smiled sadly.

"There would be war, Alan. But our government—our people—do not look for it. They are like the peeta bird, that hides its head under its wing when it is threatened."

The time of sleep was now nearly over, and we thought it best that the girls should fly back at once, so that their arrival at the city would cause as little comment as possible.

Mercer and I seated ourselves on the platform as before; the twenty girls grasped its handles, raising it until they were all upon their feet; then, at a signal, we left the ground. The trip back seemed shorter than coming up. The girls all left the valley together, flying up helter-skelter, and circling about us as we flew steadily onward.

Near the Great City the girls spread out, so as to approach it from different directions and thus attract less attention, although the time of sleep was not yet over and we knew that few would be stirring about the city.

When we reached home we greeted Lua, and dismissed the girls, arranging that they were to come back again that evening—fifty of them this time—to carry the larger platform we were to build. We then had breakfast, and after telling Lua the result of the meeting—at which she was greatly pleased—we went immediately to bed, for we were worn out.

It was about noon, I suppose, when we awoke. Mercer and I spent the afternoon building the platform on which to carry Tao's men—a framework with fifty handles instead of twenty. Miela and Anina disappeared for the whole afternoon. I did not know what they were doing at the time; later I found out Anina was devoting it to learning English.

During the evening meal we planned it all. Tao's men were living in a house near the edge of the city—the house Tao had occupied before he was banished to the Twilight Country. It had no other occupants at this time.

We had learned where they kept their boats in one of the bayous near by, and in it we intended to take them to the sea, where we would meet the girls, who would then fly with them to the Twilight Country. But we could not figure out how to capture them without alarming the city. We were sure they were unarmed; they had been carefully searched by the authorities when they entered the country. But they were ten to our two.

THE FIRE PEOPLE

Mercer voiced the problem most emphatically.

"Ten men in a house," he declared. "Maybe we can catch them all asleep. But even if they are, how are we going to get them out? There'd be a row, and we don't want any noise. Besides, there's always this confounded daylight here. If we tied them up somebody might see us when we got outside. How do we get them out of that house without any rumpus, and down to that boat? That's what I don't see."

"I—do—that," said Anina suddenly.

She had spoken in English, and we looked at her in amazement. She lisped the words in her soft, sweet voice, haltingly, like a little child. Then she turned to Miela and poured out a torrent of her native language. Mercer stared at her in undisguised admiration.

As Miela explained it, Anina proposed that she go into Tao's house alone, and decoy his men down to the boat where we could capture them.

"But how will she get them there?" I exclaimed. "What will she tell them?"

"She says she can make them think she is one of those few of our women who sympathize with their cause," Miela explained. "And she will say that the earth-man who escaped from them she has seen lurking about their boat; perhaps he plans to steal it. She will go there with them, and they can recapture him."

"They might not all go," said Mercer. "We want to get them all."

"It is Anina's thought that they will all go, for they fear this earth-man much—and all would go to make sure of him."

I could not feel it was right for us to let Anina do so daring a thing, and Mercer agreed with me heartily. But Anina insisted, with a fire in her eyes and flushed cheeks that contrasted strangely with her usually gentle demeanor.

In the end Mercer and I gave in, for we could think of no better plan, and Miela was confident Anina would not be harmed.

It was about what would correspond with ten o'clock in the evening on earth when the girls began to arrive. We waited until all fifty of them had come in. Miela named a place on the shore of the sea known to them all. They were to take the platform—starting in about two hours, when the city would be quiet—and there they would wait for us to join them in the boat.

We four started out together, but soon Anina left us to make her way to Tao's house alone. Mercer, Miela and I then hurried as fast as we could through the city down to the marshlands, and to the secluded spot on the bayou's bank where the boat was lying.

92

The bayou here was about a hundred feet wide, a winding, brackish stream, lined on both sides with trees whose roots were in the water and whose branches at times nearly met overhead. Its banks were a tangled mass of tree roots, huge ferns, palmettos and some tall upstanding kind of water grass. Half submerged logs jutted out into the sluggish current, making it in places seem almost impassable.

A narrow metal boat—a very long and very narrow motor boat with a thatched shelter like a small cabin over part of its length—lay fastened to a tree near at hand. I noticed at once some mechanism over its stern.

We had come up quietly to make sure no one was about. Now we hid ourselves close to the boat and waited with apprehension in our hearts for the arrival of Anina with Tao's men.

Half an hour, perhaps, went by. The silence in this secluded spot hung heavy about us. A fish broke the glassy surface of the water; a lizard scurried along the ground; a bird flitted past. Then, setting our hearts pounding, came the soft snapping of underbrush that we knew was the cautious tread of some one approaching. I was half reclining under a fallen tree, with a clump of palmettos about me. I parted their fronds carefully before my face. A few yards away a man was standing motionless, staring past me and apparently listening intently.

He moved forward after a moment. I feared he was coming almost upon us, but he turned aside, bending low down as he crept slowly forward. Sounds in the underbrush reached me now from other directions, and I knew that the men had spread apart and were stalking the boat, expecting Mercer to be in or near it.

Had they all come down here? I wondered. And where was Anina? I looked down at Miela warningly as I felt her move slightly.

"We'll wait till they're all near the boat," I whispered to Mercer.

I saw Anina a moment later soaring over the bayou just above the tree -tops. I sighed with relief, for it was a signal to us that everything was all right. We continued to wait until the men had all come into view. They went at the boat with a sudden rush. Several of them climbed into it, With shouts to the others.

With a significant glance to Mercer I leaped suddenly to my feet. I was perhaps twenty feet from the boat, and the space between us was fairly clear. A single bound landed me beside it, almost among four of the men who were standing there in a group. Before they had time to face me I was upon them.

I scattered them like nine -pins, and two of them went down under my blows. The other two flung themselves upon me. I stumbled over some inequality of the ground, and we all three fell prone. This was the first time I had come actually to hand grips with any of the Mercutians.

I felt now not only their lack of strength, but a curious frailness about their bodies—a seeming absence of solidity that their stocky appearance belied. These two men were like half-grown boys in my hands. I was back on my feet in a moment, leaving one of them lying motionless. The other rose to his knees, his face white with pain and terror.

I left him there and looked about me. Miela was fluttering around near by, as I had instructed her—just off the ground and with the whole scene under her eyes. It was she on whom I depended for warning should any of the quarry attempt to escape us.

At the edge of the water another man was lying, whom I assumed Mercer had felled. There was a great commotion from the boat. I ran toward it. A man was standing beside it—an old man with snow-white hair. He stood still, seeming confused and in doubt what to do. As I neared him he turned clumsily to avoid me. I passed him by and bounded over the boat's gunwale, landing in its bottom. The first thing I saw was Mercer struggling to his feet with four of the Mercutians hanging on him. One had a grip on his throat from behind; another clutched him about the knees.

The two others let go of him when they heard me land in the boat. One had evidently had enough, for he dived overboard. The other waited warily for my onslaught. As I got within reach I hit at his face, but my blow went wild. He hit me full in the chest, but it was the blow of a child.

At that instant I heard Mercer give a choking cry, and out of the corner of my eye saw him go down again. I could waste no more time upon this single antagonist. The man had his hands at my throat now. I seized him about the waist and carried him to the gunwale. He clung to me as a rat might cling to a terrier, but I shook him off and dumped him in the water.

I turned to Mercer just as he was struggling to his feet again, and in a moment more between us we had felled his two assailants. Mercer's face was very white, and I saw blood streaming from a wound on his head; but he grinned as he faced me.

"Have we—got 'em—all?" he gasped. He dashed the blood away from his eyes with the flat of his hand. "I fell—damn it—right at the start, and hit my head. Where are they all? Have we got 'em?"

Miela alighted in the boat beside us.

"Two are running," she said. "They are together. Hasten."

We jumped out of the boat. Miela flew up, and we followed her guidance through the dense woods. We could make much better speed, I knew, than the Mercutians. "We'll get them all, Ollie," I shouted at Mercer. "They're not far ahead. See up there—Miela's evidently over them now."

We came up to them after a few hundred yards. It was the old man, and one of those whom I had first encountered. They did not wait for us to attack them, but stopped stock still, flinging their arms wide in token of surrender.

Miela came down among us, and we went back to where we had lain hidden in the palmettos. There we had left a number of short lengths of rope. While we were tying the arms of these two prisoners behind them and fettering their ankles so they could not run Anina joined us.

"Two—in water," she cried; and then added something to Miela.

"Two were in the water. Now they are in the woods, running. Anina will show you."

Miela stood guard in the boat over our first two prisoners, while Mercer and I rounded up the others. It was half an hour or more before we had them all trussed up, but none of the ten escaped. We were a long time reviving two of those we had injured, but finally we had them all lying or sitting in the boat.

Mercer's head had stopped bleeding. He washed it, and I found his injury no more than an ugly scalp wound.

"I fell and cut it on something," he explained lugubriously. "Couldn't see for the blood in my eyes. But we got 'em, didn't we?"

Under Miela's direction Mercer and I shoved the boat out into the stream. I need not go into details regarding the propelling mechanism of this craft. Miela explained it hastily to me as we got under way. It used a form of the light -ray from a sort of strange battery. The intense heat of the ray generated a great pressure of superheated steam in a thick metal cylinder underneath the keel.

This steam escaped through a nozzle under water at the stern of the boat, and its thrust against the water propelled the boat forward. The boat was constructed to draw very little water, and when going fast its bow planed upward until only the stern of the hull touched the surface. It was steered by a rudder not much different from some of those types we are familiar with on earth. When we got out into open water I found the boat was capable of great speed. This I attributed not so much to the efficacy of its propelling force as to the lightness of the boat itself. It was built of some metal that I may perhaps compare with aluminium, only this was far stronger and lighter. The boat was, in fact, a mere shell, extraordinarily buoyant.

Miela sat in the stern, steering and operating the mechanism. I sat with her. Mercer was farther forward, beside Anina, talking to her earnestly. Our prisoners lay huddled in various attitudes—frightened, all of them, and obviously in no condition to give us further trouble. They were, I saw now, not ruffians by any means, but rather men of superior intelligence, selected by Tao evidently as those best fitted for spreading his propaganda among the people of the Great City.

We made slow progress down the bayou. Some of its turns were so sharp and so overhung with trees, and obstructed by fallen logs, we could hardly get through. During the latter part of the trip the bayou broadened rapidly, dividing into many channels like a delta.

We came out into the open sea finally—a broad, empty expanse, with a mirrorlike surface. The curvature of the planet was even more apparent now; it seemed almost as though the water should be sliding back downhill over the horizon.

We turned to the left as we came out of the delta, and for the first time Miela put the boat to the limit of its speed. The best comparison I can make, I think, to this rapid, noiseless, smooth progress, is that of sailing on an iceboat.

We sped along some five or ten miles, keeping close inland. I saw some of the small thatched shacks along here, though not many. For a while the shore remained that same palm -lined, half -inundated marshland. Then gradually it began to change, and we came upon a broad beach of white sand.

We landed here, and found the girls with the platform waiting for us. Miela took Anina and one or two of the older girls aside, and gave them last instructions.

"What do I do—just dump them on the other shore?" Mercer asked me.

"That's about it. I don't know the lay of the land over there. Anina does. You do what she tells you."

"You bet I will," he agreed enthusiastically. "Some kid—that little girl. We get along fine. She understands everything I say to her already. I'll have her talking English like a streak by the time you see her again."

We had removed the cords from our prisoners' ankles. I motioned them to get out of the boat. We crowded Tao's men on the platform. They were surprised, and some of them alarmed, when they saw how we proposed to transport them over the water. Miela silenced their protests, and soon we had them all seated on the platform, with Mercer at the rear end facing them.

The fifty girls grasped the platform handles. Another moment and they were in the air, with Mercer waving good -by to us vigorously.

Miela and I, left alone, watched them silently as they dwindled to a speck in the haze of the sky.

We were about to start back when we saw a girl coming toward us, flying low over the water. One of those we had directed to patrol the coast, Miela said when she came closer. She saw us, and came down on the beach.

The two girls spoke together hurriedly.

"Tao's men in the Water City have caused great disturbance, Alan," Miela said to me.

"Where's the Water City?"

"Near the Great City—across the marshlands. We must get back. And when Anina and our friend Ollie have returned we must go to the Water City. It is very bad there, she said."

Our trip back to the Great City was without unusual incident. We followed the main route at the best speed we could make.

"We shall tell our king, of course, about this disturbance," said Miela. "Perhaps he will think there is something he can do. But I fear greatly that unless he appeals directly to the people, and they are with him—"

"He's an old man," I said, "and all his councilors are old. They're not fit to rule at such a time as this. Suppose he were to die—what would happen? Who would be king then?"

"A little prince there is—a mere child. And there is our queen—a younger woman, only married to our king these few years. His first queen died."

I questioned Miela concerning her government. It was, I soon learned, an autocracy in theory. But of later years the king's advanced age, and his equally old councilors whom he refused to change, had resulted in a vacillating policy of administration, which now, I could see plainly, left the government little or no real power.

Only by constantly pandering to the wishes of the people could the king hold his throne. The supreme command was held by the king and his aged councilors. At stated intervals the more prominent men of each city met and enacted laws. The cities were each ruled by a governor in similar fashion, paying tribute to the central government somewhat after our old feudal system; but for practical purposes they acted as separate nations. They were united merely by the bonds of their common need of defense against the Twilight People, and of intermarriage, which was frequent, since the virgins, flying about, often found mates in cities other than their own.

There were courts in each city, not much more than rude tribunals, and jails in which the offenders were held. The police I have already mentioned. They, like the king's guards, were inclined in an emergency to do, not so much what they were ordered, as what they thought the people wished.

It was all very extraordinary, but like many another makeshift government it served, after a fashion.

Hiding the boat in another bayou, we took our way home on foot. That is to say, I ran, and Miela followed me, alternately flying and walking. We made our best speed this way, and very soon were back at home in the Great City.

We crossed the garden and entered the front door, expecting to find Lua in the living room, but she was not there. The house was quiet.

"She would wait up, she told me," Miela said, and, raising her voice, called her mother's name.

There was no answer, although now I remember I thought I heard a footfall upstairs.

We went up to Lua's room hurriedly. It was empty, and our loud cries of anxiety throughout the house evoked no response. We entered our own bedroom, and before I could make a move to defend myself I was seized tightly by both elbows from behind.

At the same instant an arm hooked around my neck under my chin and jerked my head backward, and another pair of arms clutched me around the knees. I struggled vainly to free myself, shouting to Miela to run.

But there were too many holding me. A moment more and my arms were tied behind me and a rope was about my legs. I was pushed into a chair, and as I sat down I saw Miela standing quietly near by, with two Mercutians holding her by the arms and shoulders.

The man who had pushed me to the seat bent down and struck me across the cheek with the flat of his hand. His grinning, malevolent face was only a few inches from mine. I saw that it was Baar!

REVOLUTION

There seemed to be five of our captors, all of them as evil-looking men as I think I have ever seen. They rummaged about the room, evidently in search for weapons they thought I might have secreted. Then they ordered me to stand up, and without more ado led Miela and me from the house.

This was once when I was glad of the interminable daylight. I hoped we might find some early risers about the streets, for I thought certainly the time of sleep must now be nearly over. But no one was in sight as we left the garden. We turned the first corner and headed toward the base of the mountain.

"To Baar's house they are taking us, I think. It is on the marshland below." Miela spoke without fear of our captors understanding the English words. We took advantage of this until after a moment we were roughly ordered to be quiet.

Lua, we thought, must have been taken away before we arrived; we would find her at Baar's house when we arrived there. We had come down to the level marshlands now, the outskirts of the city, and were passing along a path between occasional shacks. Before us, standing alone in a rice paddy, I saw a larger, more pretentious house—a wooden structure on stilts, with a thatched roof, which Miela said was where Baar lived.

We went in single file up its board incline, and entered a squalid room with matting on the floor, a rude charcoal brazier at one side, and the remains of a previous meal lying on a table.

Two women were in the room as we entered. I took these to be Baar's wife and a servant. Two naked little children lay on the floor, one of them crying lustily.

Baar glanced around as he came in, and with what I took to be an oath ordered the children removed from the room. The slave woman—I could see she was a slave by the band upon her arm—picked them up. Evidently she did not move fast enough to suit Baar's temper, for as she straightened up the man cuffed her upon the head. She stumbled to one side against Baar's wife, who was standing there, and the other woman, with a sharp imprecation, struck her full in the breast.

Neither of them saw the look she gave as she shuffled away, carrying the infants; but I did. It was a look of the most intense hatred, born and nourished, I realized, by long ill-treatment.

THE FIRE PEOPLE

Miela and I were now bound securely hand and foot, and Miela's wings were lashed to her body. Thus rendered entirely helpless, we were laid together in a corner.

From the talk that followed Miela gathered that Baar and his men were expecting the arrival of others. He roughly ordered his wife—a woman of the Twilight Country, obviously—to clear away the remains of their last meal and bring other food. She obeyed submissively.

This, the first of the Twilight Country People I had seen, was a thick-set woman of perhaps thirty-five, although she might have been older, for her black hair, which fell in an unkempt mass to her waist, was beginning to gray. She wore a single garment, a pair of silken trousers, drab with dirt. Her clipped wings were covered in the usual way.

I could see now why Miela had said these Twilight women could not fly, for this woman's torso was fat and flabby. Her skin was curiously pale—a dead, unpleasant white. Her face was broad, heavy and unintelligent. Her eyes were large and protruded slightly.

Baar and his men ate breakfast, paying no further attention to Miela and me. Suddenly Miela spoke in a frightened whisper. "They are going now in a moment to the castle. The king they will kill!"

It was evidently a widespread plot we now overheard. Baar's followers had for some time been talking quietly with the lower classes, and, finding they could count on their support, planned now to murder the king. Then with the queen and the little prince held as hostages, they expected that the men of science, threatened also with a revolt of the peons, would release the light-ray.

The light-ray once in his control, Baar could make himself king. It seemed an absurd hope, but such was the plan they were now discussing. And what was far worse, I could see no way by which I could prevent the attempt.

"They are going to the castle—now—to murder the king?" I whispered, incredulous.

"Yes," Miela answered. "So they plan. Now—in a moment—before the time of sleep is over."

"Isn't he guarded? Can they get in the castle without arousing others?"

"There are the guards—a few. But Baar has promised them great wealth, and they will stand aside and let him pass. So it is arranged."

The arrival of several other men interrupted our whispered conversation. Baar, his meal over, consulted with them hurriedly. He then instructed his wife to watch us, and after a moment they all left the house.

The woman, who was now the only occupant of the room with us, shuffled about, clearing away the meal. I tried desperately to work my hands loose; I even tried with my teeth to gnaw Miela's bonds, but without success. Every moment counted, if we were to do anything to save the king. I wondered again where Lua was—perhaps in another part of the house here, bound as we were.

"Miela," I whispered, "ask for food. Tell her we have had nothing for many hours. Perhaps she will loosen our bonds a little to let us eat. We may be able to do something then."

The woman answered Miela's pleading by setting us up side by side, with our backs against the wall. She placed food before us, and then, with a knife, cut the cords that bound our arms.

My heart leaped exultantly; but, instead of leaving us and going on with her work, she sat down just out of reach, holding the knife in her hand and watching us narrowly.

"We must eat, Miela," I said, using as casual a tone as I could and pointing to the food smilingly. "Eat, and pretend not to notice her. Perhaps I can get to my feet."

We ate the food she had given us. I tensed the muscles of my legs, and believed that, bound as I was, I might be able to leap forward and reach the woman. It was almost hopeless to attempt it, for I realized she would meet my body with the dagger point.

We were still eating, and I was thinking over this plan, when the slave woman appeared silently in a doorway across the room, behind the woman who faced us. Something in her attitude made me look away again casually and go on with my eating.

Miela had evidently not noticed her.

The slave woman came slowly toward us. A moment later she hurled herself upon Baar's wife from behind. At the same instant I threw myself forward, falling prone, but within reach of the seated woman. I gripped her with my hands, fumbling to catch her wrists, but before I could succeed she toppled forward and fell partly over me.

THE FIRE PEOPLE

I heard Miela give a cry of fright. I struggled free and raised myself up to a half-sitting position. Baar's wife lay beside me dead, with the slave woman's knife buried to the hilt in her back.

Reaching over, I took the knife from the dead woman's fingers, and with it cut the cords that bound my ankles. I sprang to my feet. The slave had retreated and stood shrinking against the side of the room, terrified at what she had done. I paid no more attention to her for the moment, but hastened to release Miela.

We searched the house hurriedly, calling to Lua; but she did not answer, nor could we find her. When we returned the slave woman was still standing where we had left her, staring with horrified eyes at the body of her mistress.

"Tell her what she did was right," I said. "She may have saved the king. Tell her to go to your house and wait for us."

The woman nodded eagerly when Miela told her what to do, and fell on her knees before us.

"She says she will serve us always. She has been very badly treated, Alan."

We sent the woman away, and with a last hasty glance around hurriedly left the house alone with its single dead occupant. A large wooden mortar and pestle, used for pounding rice, stood in the kitchen. I carried the pestle away with me; it was nearly five feet long and quite heavy—an excellent weapon.

We hastened up through the city—Miela half walking, half flying, and I carrying this bludgeon and running with twelve-foot strides. But it was now hardly more than three-quarters of an hour since we had passed this way before, and there were still few people about to see us. Baar and his men had started some twenty minutes before us, I figured, and we must reach the castle before them.

I made extraordinary progress over the level country. But I could not run uphill for long, and soon had to slow down to a walk. Miela kept closer to me now. We approached the castle grounds.

"Where will the guards be, Miela? We must avoid them if we can. They might try to stop us."

Miela did not know where they would be; but under the circumstances, as Baar had told his men, she believed the guards would disappear from the vicinity. This conjecture proved to be correct. The guards, not wishing to be concerned in the affair at all, had simply disappeared. We saw nothing of Baar and his men on the way up the mountain, although I had hoped we might overtake them.

As we passed hurriedly through the palm gardens surrounding the castle I saw its huge front doors were closed.

"Miela, we can't get in that way. A side entrance—or some other way—"

"I know," she said. "There is a smaller door below, and others on the side."

We hastened on. Suddenly I gripped Miela by the arm.

"What's that—over there—see, beyond the grove?"

There seemed to be furtive figures lurking among the palms.

"Those cannot be Baar's men, Miela—there are too many. What can it—"

We had reached a little doorway under the front terrace. There was no time to investigate these advancing figures. Baar and his men might already be inside the castle.

I slid through the doorway, every muscle tense. Miela had brought the knife from Baar's shack, and with it clenched in her hand was close beside me. I wanted to make her stay outside, where she could fly away if danger threatened, but she pleaded to follow me, and I let her come. I needed her, since I had no idea of the interior arrangements of the building.

We passed along a dim hallway and up a narrow flight of stone steps. Not a sound came to us; the interior of the castle was silent as a tomb. At the top of the steps we came almost directly into the inner patio of the building. Across a bed of tall flowers, nodding gently in a little morning breeze that swept down from above, I saw the head and shoulders of a man standing in the center of the courtyard; the lower part of his body was hidden by the flowers. I tried to duck out of sight, but he had seen me.

He was not over forty feet away. I stepped back, believing I could reach him in a single leap; but Miela held me.

"Not you, Alan. He would cry out. The noise would bring others." She raised her knife, and her eyes blazed into mine. "Never have I thought to kill a human. But now I—a woman—must kill. Stand quiet, Alan."

She flew swiftly up and poised over the man. He had started toward us. Evidently he was, so far, as anxious for silence as we, for he made no sound. I saw now he was one of those who had come to Baar's shack. His naked shoulders, his thick neck, and bullet head were all that showed above the flower stems as he plowed his way through them directly toward me; but the hand he swung aloft to aid his progress held a knife.

THE FIRE PEOPLE

He glanced up at Miela, poised in the air above him, and saw the weapon in her hand. At this new enemy he stopped, confused.

Miela swooped down at him, and he struck at her with his knife; but she avoided it with an incredibly swift turn, and a second later had passed him and was crossing the courtyard.

Round and round she flew, her great wings flapping audibly, a giant bird circling its prey. The man turned continually to face her. Several times she swooped toward him, and as swiftly avoided his blow. From every side she threatened. The man stood now bewildered, striking wild in a frenzy, as one strikes at a darting wasp. At last, with an agonized cry, he turned and ran. Instantly she dropped upon him; there was a flash of her white arm; the man's body crumpled and lay still among the flowers.

Miela was back beside me. Her breast was heaving; her eyes were full of tears; she trembled.

"A terrible thing, Alan, my husband, for a woman to do; but it had to be."

I pressed her hand with silent understanding.

"Come, Alan," she said. "They will have heard his cry. The others—we must meet them, too."

"We must get to the king. I—"

A vibrant scream rang out from the silence of the house—a man's voice, shrill with agony—then suddenly stilled.

"Good God, Miela! The king—where is he? Take me there."

She pulled me back through the doorway. A man scurried past. I leaped at him and struck him a glancing blow with the heavy wooden pestle. He stumbled to his knees. Without thought of giving quarter, I hit him again before he could rise. He sank back, senseless or dead.

Miela was ahead of me, and I ran after her along a hallway. The sound of scurrying footsteps sounded from overhead; a woman screamed.

A broad, curving stairway fronted us. I passed Miela halfway up, and, reaching the top, ran full into another man who darted from a doorway close by. The impact of my heavier body flung him backward to the floor. I leaped over him with a shout of warning to Miela, and ran on into the room.

A man was standing stock still in its center. It was Baar. He flung his knife at me as I appeared, but it went wild. Two other men were coming toward me from opposite sides of the room. I swung the bludgeon about me viciously, keeping them away. Suddenly Baar shouted a command, and before I could reach any one of them they had scurried away like rats.

A low bed with a huge canopy of silk stood against the wall. A woman knelt on the floor beside it, and against her knees huddled a little half-grown boy.

I heard Miela's voice shouting in her own language. The sound of men running came from below. Then Miela's half-hysterical laughter, and then the words: "They are running away, Alan—all of them. I have been calling you to bring me the light -ray. And they are running away."

I turned to the bed, pushing its curtains aside, and then hurriedly closing them again with a shudder.

Miela was beside me.

"The king is dead, Miela. No—you must not look."

Her eyes widened; her hand went to her breast.

"There is one who needs you." I pointed to the woman on the floor.

She was staring at us, unseeing, one arm flung about the child protectingly, holding him partially under one of her long, sleek red wings. The fingers of her other hand clutched convulsively at the bed coverings; she was moaning softly with a grief and terror all the more intense because it was restrained.

"There is one who needs you, Miela," I repeated. "Comfort her—for we have come too late."

The castle now was in thorough confusion. Several waiting maids rushed into the room, stared at their mistress and the little prince, and, seeing what had happened, stood silently wringing their hands in fright, or fled aimlessly through the halls. One of the king's councilors had come in, stopping, bewildered, at the scene that met him.

"Tell him what has occurred, Miela," I said.

There came now faintly to my ears from outside the castle sounds of a gathering crowd—murmurs and vague muffled shouts. The cries grew louder. A rain of missiles struck the castle; a stone came through a near-by window, falling almost at my feet. All at once I remembered the lurking figures we had seen among the palms in the garden.

"Miela!" I cried. "Hear that, outside! A crowd is gathering. The men we saw—out there! People whom Baar has—Miela, ask him, for God's sake, to tell us how we can get weapons. Where are the other councilors? Send for them. We must do something—now, at once. This is revolution, Miela—don't you understand? Revolution!"

I felt so impotent. Here in this crisis I could talk to no one but Miela—could issue no direct commands—could understand the words of no one but her.

Suddenly, from over our heads, a great, solemn deep-throated bell began tolling.

"What is that? What does that mean?"

A girl rushed into the room.

"It is the bell of danger," said Miela quickly. "The girls are ringing it to arouse the city. Up here then will the people hurry to find out what it is that threatens."

"They're outside now," I retorted. "Order all the king's councilors here at once. Find out if any guards are about the place. Send them here. Where is the head of the city's police? Send him here to me! Tell him to call out all his men."

What was I saying? I had forgotten the one vital thing!

"Miela! The light-ray! These men of science who guard it, where are they? Send for their leader. Get him here to me at once—we must have the ray!"

Miela stood very quietly beside me. Her face was white; her eyes blazed, but she seemed calm and unfrightened.

"He will come," she said, "and armed with the ray. The bell will bring him. Your other commands I will see are obeyed."

The old councilor, who had been standing by, dazed, came slowly forward at Miela's call. The king's councilor! And all the others were like him. The king was dead, and here was the little prince huddled in his mother's arm! Realization had been slow in coming, but now it broke upon me like a great light.

I flung the bludgeon away from me, and stood erect.

"Miela," I cried, "tell him—tell them all—their king is dead. It is I who command now. There is no one else—and I have the power. Tell them that. It is I, the man from earth, who commands!"

THE NEW RULER

The solemn bell continued pealing out its knell; the shouts and tumult outside were growing louder. Miela spoke hurriedly to the old man, then turned to leave the room.

"Your commands shall be obeyed, my husband," she said quietly.

I felt again that sudden sense of helplessness as I saw her leave.

"Be careful, Miela. Order every one in the castle to the roof. Here! Tell the queen before you go. Send every one up there with me. The mob may come in. We'll make our stand up there."

I understood Baar's plot better now. He had gathered his mob of peons to surround the castle and make a demonstration in his favor. Then, with the king dead and the queen and her little son held by him and his men—their lives as forfeits—he hoped to be able to treat with the men of science who controlled the light-ray, and who, I did not doubt, represented the better element among the people.

It seemed a mad plan at best; and now that it had gone wrong, I wondered what Baar would attempt to do. Evidently he and his henchmen had all left the castle, fearing the light-ray, which Miela pretended I held. They were outside now, among the mob, I assumed. Would the mob attempt to enter?

Miela hurried away to send every one inside the building to its roof. The queen, following Miela's commands unquestioningly, took the little prince by the hand and, signing to me to follow, led me upstairs.

There was only one stairway leading to the roof, I found with satisfaction, and it was narrow—an excellent place for defense. The roof was broad and flat, flanked at the ends by two towers which rose considerably above it.

It was a frightened little group who gathered about me—the queen and her son, two of the king's councilors, and perhaps half a dozen young girls whom I took to be the queen's attendants. Others came up each moment.

I sat the queen down on a little white stone bench in the center of the garden, and bowed before her respectfully. Then I smiled upon them all. I think they were reassured and trusted me, and I found my commands were obeyed without question.

The queen was a woman of perhaps thirty-five—tall and slender, with black hair and eyes. She was dressed in a single garment of heavy white silk, a dress that fell ungathered at the waist from above her breast under the arms to her ankles. It was, I judged, her sleeping robe. Her hair hung in two long braids over her shoulders; her feet were incased in sandals.

She was unquestionably a beautiful woman. I remember my vague surprise, as I saw her, with her son by her side, and her long sleek wings unmutilated. And then I saw that her wings were fastened together in two places by little metal chains. She, then, like other married women, was not permitted to fly, although the beauty of her wings was unspoiled.

I sent two of the old men to stand by the head of the stairs. Miela had given me her knife, and I handed it now to one of them, trying to make him understand that he was to bar the passage of any one who should not be allowed up. He shuddered, but he took the knife and stood where I indicated.

The crowd in the garden below had seen us on the roof now, and the tumult of shouts was doubled. I went to the parapet and looked over.

The garden was full of a struggling, confused mass of people. Those nearest the castle were mostly peons. I noticed men and a few women armed with various implements of agriculture, and any sort of rude weapon they could obtain. They were standing about in little groups or rushing excitedly to and fro in aimless, uncommanded activity.

Many of them held stones in their hands, which occasionally they cast at the building. It was one of those mobs that gather ready for trouble, is swayed in almost any direction by any chance leadership, and most frequently accomplishes nothing.

I felt a sudden sense of relief. The garden was rapidly filling up with men and women of the more intelligent classes, who mingled with the others, learned what had occurred—for I did not doubt but that the knowledge of the king's death had spread about—and then stood waiting to see what would happen.

The air was full of excited girls flying over the castle. A few alighted for a moment on the roof, but I did not fear them. Where was Baar? I could not hope to distinguish him among the crowd, but still I saw no sign of his leadership. Had he seen the failure of his plan and, fearing the results of his regicide, fled the vicinity? I hoped so fervently.

As I showed myself at the parapet a great shout arose. Some of the men—I knew at once it was those who had heard I possessed the light -ray—scattered in terror at my appearance. I determined then, if no issue were raised that would demand my using this supposed weapon, I could continue to command the situation.

I stood there a moment looking down. At the edge of the crowd I saw a few figures whom I took to be members of the city's police. They were standing idle, taking no part in what was going on. There seemed nothing I could do until Miela returned. If only I could speak to the crowd! I wondered if I dared descend among them and disperse the mob of peons. I went to the head of the stairway. Three or four of the king's councilors were standing there.

There was no one on the stairs; evidently every one living in the castle was now on its roof—some thirty of them altogether. The crowd outside quite evidently had no present intention of entering the building. The mob of peons Baar had gathered were greatly in the minority now, and I felt that matters were steadily improving. I wondered where Miela was, and then while I was standing there I saw her coming up the stairs, a man following close behind her.

I think I have never been so glad to see any one as I was to see her at this moment. Her face was grave; her demeanor calm, as before.

"He is here," she said as she came to the head of the stairs. "This is Fuero, Alan, leader of the men of science, who have the ray."

As he came out onto the roof I saw this man was easily the most dominant personality I had so far encountered on Mercury. He was tall for his race, although several inches shorter than I, a man of sixty, perhaps, with iron-gray hair falling long about his ears.

He wore sandals and a pair of the usual knee-length, wide-cut trousers. But what distinguished him in his dress was a broad panel of heavy silk, hanging from neck to knee, both in back and front, with an opening at the top through which his head was thrust. This silken panel was some eighteen inches wide, light gray in color, and richly embroidered in gold in various designs. It hung free, except for a slight fastening at the waist line. Beneath it the man's naked torso—and his bare arms—showed powerfully muscled.

His face was smooth shaven, with strong, regular features. I noticed, too, there was a slight cleft in his square chin. His forehead was high, his blue eyes kindly, yet with a searching, piercing quality about them.

It was not so much the man's general appearance as his bearing that made me realize he was a forceful character. There was about him unmistakable poise. I knew at once he felt his power, his authority. That he would use it wisely I could not doubt.

THE FIRE PEOPLE

He stood regarding me gravely—an appraising regard under which I felt myself flushing a little. Miela spoke to him swiftly, and he inclined his head to me by way of introduction, his glance meanwhile taking in the scene on the roof.

With Miela as interpreter we held a hurried conversation. I learned then that Fuero and his associates had many years before organized a society for the development of the light -ray in its various forms. They had soon realized in their experiments its diabolical power of destruction, and had taken oath then that they would not use it, or allow it to be used, except under the most critical circumstances of the nation's welfare.

Realizing, too, the power it gave them as individuals, they had sworn to remain men of science only, taking no part in public affairs, remaining rigidly aloof from all national affairs. Most of their work concerned the development of the light -ray for industrial purposes. In these forms it developed heat, but had very little power of projection.

All this Miela told me in a few brief sentences.

"How did Tao get the ray?" I demanded.

"Some members of the society proved false," she answered. "When Tao was banished to the Twilight Country they deserted their brothers and joined him. There were others with him of scientific mind, and these soon learned how to make it, too."

Fuero was still regarding me appraisingly. I felt suddenly very young, very inadequate as I stood there facing him. But I met his gaze squarely, and all at once he smiled.

"He says, 'Let us speak to the people,'" said Miela.

We went to the parapet. Only a few moments had elapsed since I had stood there before. The situation below was unchanged, except that the crowd had grown denser.

A sudden hush fell as they saw us. Fuero turned to me and spoke quietly; his eyes seemed searching out my thoughts.

"He asks you, my husband, if you will take oath before your God to do what is right for our people. He wishes to trust you now in this crisis, for there is no one else, and he believes in you."

"I will, Miela," I said solemnly. "Before God I swear it."

The man gazed steadily into my eyes another instant, then abruptly he thrust a small metal cylinder into my hand. I thrilled as my fingers closed around it. He seemed to hesitate, then he turned and, slowly crossing the rooftop, looking neither to right nor left, he descended the stairs out of our sight.

He had done what he thought was best, and, having done it, had withdrawn immediately from further participation in the affair.

It may have been the absence of his dominant personality, or the grasp of my hand about this little metal cylinder, but now I felt a renewed sense of responsibility, and with it a feeling of power that swept aside all doubts and all fears. Now I could command, could guide and control, the destiny of this nation, and could, thank God, save my own world.

"Miela," I said, "tell the queen her son shall be king. I am about to proclaim him king before the people, and I, as regent, will rule. Tell her that, and bring him here now to me."

The queen made no answer, save a slight inclination of her head. But I saw that she had recovered composure. She pushed her son gently away from her, and I strode forward to meet him.

"Tell him, Miela, he is a man now, and must have no fear, for he is the greatest man in all this land."

I patted his shoulder as he stood beside me, and he looked up into my face and smiled bravely.

The top of the parapet was flat and broad. I raised the little boy up and stood him upon it. Instantly another tumult of shouts arose.

I looked down and saw the figure of Fuero as he stalked unheeding across the garden, the people respectfully opening up a path before his advance.

Approval and derision seemed mingled in the cries that greeted the appearance of the little prince.

"Quiet them if you can, Miela," I said. "Speak to them."

I steadied the boy with my hand, and he stood there unafraid, a sturdy, manly little figure.

Miela raised her voice and began speaking. The shouts partially ceased, then suddenly a stone struck the parapet almost in front of us.

A sudden rage possessed me. I fumbled at the cylinder I held. It was very much like a little hand flashlight, and seemed to have a knob at my thumb. Miela stopped speaking and turned to me.

"There—press that, Alan. Careful! Aim it there! See! Over there against those palms."

THE FIRE PEOPLE

I held the thing up and pointed it toward the huge royal palms, aiming at their graceful fronds high over the heads of the people. My hand pressed the knob; the little cylinder seemed to thrill in my grasp. A tiny beam of light shot out -quite plainly visible—a green, shading into red. It struck the palm branches, and silently yet rapidly, as though they were under some giant blow -torch, they shriveled, crackled, and burst into flame.

Miela's fingers bit into my arm. "Enough, Alan! Stop!"

My thumb yielded to the upward pressure of the tiny knob against it, and abruptly the light vanished. A narrow swath had been cut through the palms—a furrow of death plowed by the pressure of my thumb against a bit of metal!

The crowd had frozen into the immobility of terror. Now, as the dreaded ray vanished as suddenly as it had sprung forth, they turned with cries of fright to escape. No one had been hurt. I shuddered as I realized now that many girls had been in the air, and through no thought or skill of mine had they escaped.

"Speak to them, Alan," Miela cried. "There must be no panic. Here must they stay and listen to what you have to say. Speak to them; stop them now."

I handed her the cylinder, lest the diabolical thing spit forth again its fire from my unskillful fingers, and leaped to the top of the parapet.

"Stop!" I shouted at the top of my voice. "Stop—all of you! At once!"

I waved my arms violently: I knew my words meant nothing, but my voice carried far. The excitement continued. But a few stopped and stared at me; then others, and gradually there was less confusion.

Miela turned and shouted something to the girls on the rooftop. Instantly they spread their wings and flew, down, circling close over the heads of the people.

"Wait, Alan. A moment now and there will be quiet. The girls are telling them not to fear, but to wait and listen to what you have to say."

Miela stood now upon the parapet top, with the little prince between us. She had concealed the tiny metal cylinder in her belt; her open palms were flung out before her, and her wings, spread and flapping slowly, raised her on tiptoe. Every line of her graceful body was tense; her attitude bespoke power, dominance, authority. And then she began to talk in a voice vibrant with emotion. Once she laid her hand lightly upon the curly head of the little boy, and a tremulous, uncertain cheer answered her from below.

"I have told them of the king's death, Alan," she said a moment later, "and that here is their little king standing before them; And now, of you—what shall I say?"

"Tell them that until the king is older, I—the man from earth—shall rule them as regent. Tell them if they obey me all will be well, for I shall rule them wisely."

I stood while Miela translated this amid dead silence from the crowd. As she finished I raised myself to full height and stared down at them threateningly.

"But if there is trouble—if any one defies my authority—then, Miela, tell them I shall use the light-ray, for I shall brook no interference."

The silence from below continued.

I spread my hands out before me and smiled.

"But there will be no trouble. I am with the Light Country, heart and soul. Its interests are my interests, for I have married one of its women, and now I too am one of its people.

"Tao shall be overthrown—tell them that, Miela. The Twilight People never again shall threaten our cities. If more land is wanted by our people of the Light Country, tell them they shall have it. All the land they desire shall be theirs. For when Tao is vanquished I shall build great cars such as he is building, and all who wish may go to my earth peacefully, and we will make them welcome as I have been made welcome here."

A cheer arose as Miela translated this; and now for the first time I heard no cries of dissent.

"Say to them again I shall rule them wisely. Say I shall look to them—all of them, rich and poor alike—for help in what we have to do. All must help me, for I am only one, and I need them all. When this work we have to do is over, when our nation is freed forever from this menace from across the sea, tell them that then I will give my every thought to the details of their welfare. All that they wish—if it lays in my power—shall be done."

A girl alighted for an instant on the parapet near me; another, darted downward in her flight, evidently to avoid the disrespect of passing directly in front of me. The thought flashed through my mind that I might mention the virgins and promise them reversal of the law they so abhorred, but I felt it would be impolitic to raise that question at such a time as this.

"Tell them now to leave the grounds, quietly," I concluded. "When I wish them again they will be sent for. All that I do will be known through public proclamation."

I lifted the little prince in my arms, and then, with the cheers of the people ringing in my ears, jumped backward with him to the roof below.

THE FIRE PEOPLE

Thus, by swift moving circumstances which could not have been foreseen, was I made ruler of the Light Country. The crowd dispersed quietly. We sent the queen and her waiting maids back to her apartments, the aged councilors to theirs, and soon Miela and I were alone in one of the castle rooms.

Now that the nervous excitement under which I had been laboring was over, I felt utterly exhausted. I dropped wearily into a seat, and Miela sat on the floor at my feet with her arms on my knees.

I stroked her glossy black hair idly.

"I'm tired, girl. I'm all in. Aren't you?"

We had not slept since the afternoon before, and so much had happened since. Suddenly I remembered Lua.

"Miela—your mother. We must find her." I started to my feet, then sat down again.

There was no use of my rushing away on some aimless search over a city like this.

"Where is the head of the city's police, Miela?"

"I have sent for him. He should be here now to see you."

"I must have him search the city. Lua must be found. The castle guards—we must appoint others, Miela. I must have a council, too—not doddering old men, but others that we shall select. Who collects the taxes? Where is the money? Who handles it?"

The questions piled upon me faster than I could voice them, and all the while my tired brain and weary, aching body called only for rest—for sleep.

I thought of Mercer and Anina. They should be back by now.

"We must send home and have them told we are here, Miela. And that slave woman of Baar's—she will be there, too. She must be sent here to us also."

We had decided to live in the castle.

"When Mercer and Anina return, we must arrange to go to the Water City. The disturbance there must be quelled. All the cities must be told of our actions here. I must visit them all, Miela."

My voice seemed trailing off as though I were talking to myself. A thousand problems rushed in confusion through my mind. I felt I was talking almost incoherently. A knock on the door of our room brought me to myself.

A young girl stood respectfully on the threshold. Miela listened to what she had to say, questioned her swiftly, and then turned to me. Her face had gone suddenly white.

"The girls have returned from over the sea, Alan. This is one of them. But Anina and our friend Ollie have stayed there."

"Stayed there?" I cried. "Why?"

"They set free Tao's men as we planned. They were on their way back when the earth-man suddenly bid Anina return. Something was wrong, he said. This girl does not understand what. But they went back. And Anina and Ollie they left there, standing on the shore together. We are to go over to the same place to-night, if we can, and get them. That is all the girl knows."

The girl withdrew after a moment.

Mercer and Anina left in the Twilight Country! Miela and I stared at each other blankly.

IN THE TWILIGHT COUNTRY

Mercer sat on the rear end of the platform and waved good -by vigorously as he was carried swiftly up and out over the water. Under him was a pile of blankets and a coat, and beside him a box of baked dough -like bread—the food he was to turn over to Tao's emissaries when he set them free.

Anina flew at his side, at intervals smiling up at him reassuringly. Before him on the platform his captives huddled. Although all of them were trussed up securely, he menacingly kept his little wooden revolver pointed at them from the level of his knee.

He chuckled as he thought of the fight at the bayou. Everything was working out all right; it was surprising what one could do with his physical strength here on Mercury.

The girls had carried the platform up some five hundred feet above the sea. Mercer turned and looked back. The shore had already dropped almost to the rim of the close -encircling horizon. He leaned over toward Anina, resting one hand on the bamboo handle she was holding. "How long will it take us to get there, Anina?"

He knew the girl would understand his words, but he did not realize she had little basis for comparing time in his language.

"Long time," she answered, smiling. "But we go quickly now."

He sat back again and waited. It seemed like hours—it was hours probably, three or four—and still they swept onward straight as an arrow.

After another interminable interval Anina raised one hand and pointed ahead. "Twilight Country—there," she said.

Mercer saw, coming up over the horizon, the dim outlines of a rocky land sparsely covered with trees. It spread out rapidly before him as he watched, fascinated. It seemed a desolate land, a line of low, barren hills off to one side, and a forest of stunted, naked -looking trees in front. The platform swept on over the shore line, a rocky beach on which the calm sea rolled up in tiny white lines of breakers. Then in a great curve the girls circled to one side.

"Where are we going?" Mercer asked.

"A trail—near us somewhere. A trail to the Lone City. There we land."

Mercer saw the trail in a moment. It came out of the woods and struck the shore by a little bight where boats could land. The girls swooped downward, and in a moment more the platform was lying motionless on the beach.

116

Mercer looked around. It was light enough to see objects in the immediate foreground—a gray twilight. The forest came almost to the water's edge. He saw now the trees might have been firs, but with small, twisted trunks, few branches except near the top, and very few leaves. They seemed somehow very naked and starved—indeed, it surprised him that they could grow at all in such a rocky waste. The end of the trail was close before him. It appeared merely an opening in the trees with the fallen logs and underbrush cleared away.

The girls were obviously cold, standing idle now after their long flight. Mercer lost no time in preparing for the return journey. He tumbled his captives unceremoniously off the platform and set the box of food and blankets beside them.

"What's this, Anina?"

He was holding in his palm a tiny metal cylinder.

Anina took it from him.

"For fire, see?"

She picked up a bit of driftwood, and, holding the end of the cylinder against it, pressed a little button. A curl of smoke rose from the wood, and in a moment a wisp of flame.

"A light-ray!" Mercer exclaimed.

"The ray—but different."

She tossed the blazing bit of wood aside, and held her hand a foot or so in front of the cylinder.

"No danger! See?" She brought her hand closer. "Heat here—close—no heat far away."

Mercer understood then that this was not a light-ray projector, but a method of producing heat with the property of radiation, but not of projection—a different and harmless form of the ray.

He took the little cylinder from the girl, inspected it curiously, then laid it on the blankets.

"They'll need it, I guess, if it's any colder where they're going."

He set one of the captives free.

"Anina, tell him to sit quiet until we've gone. Then he can cut the others loose." He tossed a knife into the box. "Come on, Anina; let's get away."

They were about ready to start back, when Mercer suddenly decided he was hungry. He hopped off the platform. "They don't need all that food."

He gathered some of the little flat cakes of dough in his hands. "Want some?" He offered them to the girls, who smilingly refused.

"All right. I do. I'm hungry. Might as well take a blanket, too. It's devilish cold."

He was back on the platform in a moment, sitting down with the blanket about his knees and munching contentedly at the bread.

"All right, Anina. Start her off."

They swung up into the air and began the return flight.

A few hours more and they would be back at the Great City. Then the real work would begin. Mercer squared his shoulders unconsciously as he thought of all there was to do.

But there was no danger to the Light Country from Tao, he thought with satisfaction. At least, there would be none when the other cities were rid of Tao's men, as the Great City was now. The men would find their way back all right—

At the sudden thought that came to him Mercer dropped his bit of bread and sat up in astonishment. Tao no longer a menace? He remembered my reasoning in the boat coming down the bayou. Of course, Tao would have no reason to attack the Light Country by force of arms until he was sure his propaganda among the people had failed.

My argument was sound enough, but the utter stupidity of what we had done now dawned on Mercer with overwhelming force. Tao would await the results of his emissaries' work, of course. And here we had gone and sent them straight back to their leader to report their efforts a failure! If anything were needed to precipitate an invasion from Tao, this very thing Mercer had just finished doing was it. He cursed himself and me fervently as he thought what fools we had been.

Then it occurred to him perhaps it was not too late to repair the damage. Not more than half an hour had passed since he had set the men free on the shore of the Twilight Country. He must go back at once. Under no circumstances must they be allowed to reach Tao and tell him what had occurred.

Anina was flying near Mercer as before. He leaned over the edge of the platform to talk with her, but the wind of their forward flight and the noise of the girls' wings made conversation difficult.

"Anina! Come up here with me. Sit here. I want to talk to you. It's important. They don't need you flying now."

Obediently the girl sat where he indicated, close beside him. And then as he was about to begin telling her what was in his mind Mercer suddenly remembered that they were still heading toward the Light Country, every moment getting farther away from Tao's men, whose homeward journey he must head off some way.

"We must go back, Anina—back where we came from—at once. Tell them—now! Then I'll tell you why."

The girl's eyes widened, but she did as he directed, and the platform, making a broad, sweeping turn, headed back toward the Twilight Country shore.

"Anina, how far is it to Tao's city from where we landed?"

"The Lone City? A day, going fast."

"But they won't go fast, will they? Some of them are pretty badly hurt."

"Two days for them," the girl agreed.

Mercer then told her what an error we had made. She listened quietly, but he knew she understood, not only his words, but the whole situation as he viewed it then.

"Most bad," she said solemnly when he paused.

"That's what I want to tell you; it's bad," he declared. "We've got to head them off some way; stop them somehow. I don't see how we're going to capture them again—ten of them against me. But we've got to do something."

Then he asked her about the lay of the country between the shore of the sea and the Lone City.

Anina's English was put to severe test by her explanation; but she knew far many more words than she had ever used, and now, with the interest of what she had to say, she lost much of the diffidence which before had restrained her.

She told him that the trail led back through the forest for some distance, and then ran parallel with a swift flowing river. This river, she explained, emptied into the Narrow Sea a few miles below the end of the trail. It was the direct water route to the Lone City.

The trail, striking the river bank, followed it up into a mountainous country—a metallic waste where few trees grew. There was a place still farther up in a very wild, broken country, where the river ran through a deep, narrow gorge, and the trail followed a narrow ledge part way up one of its precipitous sides.

Anina's eyes sparkled with eagerness as she told of it.

"There, my friend Ollie, we stop them. Many loose stones there are, and the path is very narrow."

Mercer saw her plan at once. They could bar the men's passage somewhere along this rocky trail, and with stones drive them back. He realized with satisfaction that he could throw a stone fully twice as large and twice as far as any of the men, and thus, out of range, bombard them until they would be glad enough to turn back.

His plan, then, was to land, and with Anina follow the men. The rest of the girls he would send back to me with the platform, to tell Miela and me to come over the next evening to the end of the trail.

He and Anina meanwhile would keep close behind the men, and then when the cañon was neared, get around in front of them, and bar their farther advance. This would be easy since he could walk and run much faster than they, and Anina could fly. He would drive them back out of the gorge, send Anina to keep the appointment with me and bring me up to him with the girls and the platform.

They reached the shore and landed within a few feet of where they had been an hour before. The men were not in sight; nothing remained to show they had been there, save pieces of cut cord lying about.

Anina now instructed the girls what to tell me, and in a moment more, with the blanket and a few pieces of bread, she and Mercer were left standing alone on the rocky beach. Anina was cold. He took off his fur jacket and wrapped it about her shoulders.

She made a quaint little picture standing there, with her two long braids of golden hair, and her blue -feathered wings which the jacket only partly covered. They started up the trail together. It was almost dark in the woods, but soon their eyes grew accustomed to the dim light, and they could see a little better. They walked as rapidly, as Anina was able, for the men had nearly an hour's start, and Mercer concluded they would be far ahead.

They had gone perhaps a mile, climbing along over fallen logs, walking sometimes on the larger tree trunks lying prone—rude bridges by which the trail crossed some ravine—when Anina said: "I fly now. You wait here, Ollie, and I find where they are."

She handed him the coat and flew up over the tree -tops, disappearing Almost immediately in the darkness. Mercer slung the coat around him and sat down to wait. He sat there perhaps fifteen or twenty minutes, staring up at the silent, motionless tree -tops, and thinking all sorts of vague, impossible dangers impending. Then he heard her wings flapping and saw her flitting down through the trees.

"Very near, they are," she said as soon as she reached the ground. "A fire—they have—and they are ready now to sleep."

They went on slowly along the trail, and soon saw the glimmer of a fire ahead. "A camp for the night," whispered Mercer.

"It must be nearly morning now."

He looked about him and smiled as he realized that no light would come with the morning. Always this same dim twilight here—and eternal darkness on ahead. "Good Lord, what a place to live!" he muttered.

They crept on cautiously until they were within sight of the camp. A large fire was burning briskly. Most of the men were wrapped in their blankets, apparently asleep; three were sitting upright, on guard. Mercer and Anina crept away.

"We'd better camp, too," Mercer said when they were well out of hearing. "They will probably stay there four or five hours, anyway. Lord, I'm tired." He laid his hand on her shoulder gently, almost timidly. "Aren't you tired, too, little girl?"

"Yes," she answered simply, and met his eyes with her gentle little smile. "Oh, yes—I tired. Very much."

They did not dare light a fire, nor had they any means of doing so. They went back from the trail a short distance, finding a little recess between two fallen logs, where the ground was soft with a heavy moss. Here they decided to sleep for a few hours.

A small pool of water had collected on a barren surface of rock near by, and from this they drank. Then they sat down, together and ate about half the few remaining pieces of bread which Mercer was carrying in the pockets of his jacket. They were both tired out. Anina particularly was very sleepy.

When they had finished eating Anina lay down, and Mercer covered her with the blanket. She smiled up at him.

"Good night, Anina."

"Good night, my friend Ollie."

She closed her eyes, snuggling closer under the blanket with a contented little sigh. Mercer put on his jacket and sat down beside her, his chin cupped in his hand. It seemed colder now. His trousers were thin, his legs felt numb and stiff from his recent exertion.

He sat quiet, staring at the sleeping girl. She was very beautiful and very sweet, lying there with her golden hair framing her face, her little head pillowed on her arms, a portion of one blue-feathered wing peeping out from under the blanket. All at once Mercer bent over and kissed her lightly, brushing her lips with his, as one kisses a sleeping child.

She stirred, then opened her eyes and smiled up at him again.

"You cold, Ollie," she said accusingly. She lifted an edge of the blanket. "Here—you sleep, too."

He stretched himself beside her, and she flung a corner of the blanket over him; and thus, like two children lost in the woods and huddled together for warmth under a fallen log, they slept.

ANOTHER LIGHT -RAY!

The news that Mercer and Anina had been left in the Twilight Country completely dumfounded Miela and me. "Something was wrong," Mercer had said. And then they had insisted on staying there, and had sent the girls back to tell me to come over.

We could make nothing of it, nor did the half hour of argument into which we immediately plunged further enlighten us. That flaw in our plans which had dawned on Mercer so suddenly and clearly certainly never occurred to us, for all it was seemingly so obvious.

We were interrupted—having reached no conclusion whatever except that we would go over that evening as Mercer had directed—by the arrival of the police chief to see me. He was a little man, curiously thin and wizened for a Mercutian, with wide pantaloons, a shirt, short jacket and little triangular cocked hat. His face seemed pointed, like a ferret. His movements were rapid, his roving glance peculiarly alert.

He bowed before me obsequiously. He would obey me to the letter, I could see that at once from his manner; though, had I impressed him as being like my predecessor, I did not doubt but that he would do as he pleased upon occasion.

I toyed with the little light -ray cylinder in my hand quite casually through the brief interview, and I saw he was thoroughly impressed, for he seemed unable to take his eyes from it.

"Where are your men just now?" I asked.

He raised his hands deprecatingly and poured out a flood of words to Miela when my question was translated to him.

"He himself was sleeping," she said to me when he had paused for breath. "His third watch was on patrol about the city. Then from the castle came the king's guards, fleeing in haste. Those of the police they met they told that evil men were in the castle with the light -ray, and all who represented the city's authority would be killed."

"That was a lie," I interrupted. "There was no light -ray here then."

Miela nodded. "It was what Baar's men had told them to say, I think."

"And then what happened to the police?"

"Then they left their posts about the city. Some fled; others went back and reported what they had heard."

123

"And it never occurred to any of them to come up here and try to stop the disturbance? Curious policemen, these!"

"It is too deadly—the light -ray," said Miela. "They were afraid. And then the alarm bell began ringing. They sent for Ano, here, to ask him what they should do. And then you sent for him. He has his men at the police building, in waiting. And he comes to you at the risk of his life, and now asks your commands."

Thus did my chief of police explain satisfactorily to himself, and with great protestations of loyalty to his trust, how it came about that he and his men did nothing while their king was being murdered and another put in his place.

Recriminations seemed useless. He stood bowing and scraping before me, eager only to obey my slightest wish.

"Tell him, Miela, how Baar's men captured Lua. Have the city, thoroughly searched—Baar's house particularly. Tell him I killed Baar's wife. Have that slave woman sent home to me.

"Tell him to capture Baar and any of his known associates. If he does, have him report to me at once. Say to him that I must have word of Lua—or I'll have a new chief of police by to -morrow. For the rest, have his men patrol the city as usual."

I spoke as sternly as I could, and the little man received my words with voluble protestations of extreme activity on his part.

When he had bowed himself out I smiled at Miela hopelessly.

"This has got to be a mighty different government before we can ever hope to accomplish anything against Tao." Tao was not worrying me for the moment. Lua must be found, and I had no idea of relying entirely upon this little chief of police to find her. And Mercer needed me, too, this very evening.

I stood up wearily and put my arm about Miela's shoulders. Her little body drooped against mine, her head resting on my shoulder. There was little about us then, as we stood there dispirited and physically tired out, that would have commended respect from our subjects.

"We must get some sleep, Miela," I said. "Things will look very different to us then."

It must have been mid -afternoon when we awoke. Ano was at hand to report that Baar and his men, and all the king's guards, must have fled the city. Of Lua he had, so far, found no trace. Baar's slave woman was in the castle, waiting our commands. The girl who had brought us Mercer's message was also waiting to ask us when we wanted her and the other girls for the trip back to the Twilight Country.

"Right away," I exclaimed. "I'm not going to take any chances with Mercer. We'll start at once."

The girl flew away to get her friends and the platform, which had been left in the garden of Miela's home. I planned to start openly from the castle roof; there was now no need of maintaining secrecy.

The disappearance of Lua was alarming. Equally so was the possible danger into which Mercer might have blundered. In Lua's case there did not seem much I could do personally at that moment. Before starting I arranged with the aged councilors to call a meeting the following morning of all government officials.

"Could we get Fuero to come, Miela?"

She shook her head positively. "His oath would forbid it."

"Well, tell the councilors to call also any of the city's prominent men. I've got to get some good men with me. I can't do it all alone."

Miela smiled at me quizzically as I said this: "You have forgotten our women and their help, my husband?"

I had, in very truth, for the moment.

"We'll need them, too," I said. "Tell these girls who carry us to-night to call all those who went with us to the mountains—a meeting to-morrow at this time—here on the castle roof."

"To the Water City we must go," Miela said. "There Tao's men are very strong, our girls report. And to-day there was a fight among the people, and several were killed."

"But we must go armed, Miela, with more than one light-ray. I shall see this Fuero to-morrow. After all, he's the key-note to the whole thing."

We started from the castle roof, Miela sitting with me this time on the platform. Flying low, we passed over the maze of bayous, and in what seemed an incredibly short time we were out over the sea. I had now no idea what we might be called upon to do, or how long we would be gone, for all my specific plans for the next day; so we started as well prepared as possible.

The precious light-ray cylinder I held in my hand. We had a number of blankets, enough food for us all for two days of careful rationing, a knife or two, and a heavy, sharp-edged metal implement like an ax.

It seemed hardly more than half an hour before a great black cloud had spread over the whole sky, and we ran into the worst storm I have ever encountered. The wind came up suddenly, and we fought our way directly into it. Lightning flashed about us, and then came the rain, slanting down in great sheets.

We were still flying low. The mirror surface of the sea was now lashed with waves, extraordinarily high, whose white tops blew away in long streaks of scud. The girls fought sturdily against the wind and rain, carrying us steadily up until after a while I could not see the water below.

We were in the storm perhaps an hour altogether. Then we passed up and beyond it; and emerged again into that gray vacancy, with a waste of storm-lashed water far beneath us.

The Twilight Country shore was still below the horizon, and it was a considerable time before we sighted it. Miela and I sat quiet, wrapped in a blanket, which, wet as it was, offered some protection against the biting wind. The girls seemed exhausted from their long struggle against the storm, and I was glad for them when we finally landed.

This was the place, they said, where Mercer and Anina had set Tao's men free, and where the two were standing when the girls had left with the platform. I looked about, and saw on the beach the pieces of cut cord with which the men had been bound.

Of Mercer and Anina there was no sign. We waited until well after the time of the evening meal, and still Mercer and Anina did not arrive. We concluded, of course, that they had followed Tao's men up the trail for some reason, and we expected it would be Anina who would come back to tell us where Mercer was.

"Let us go up a little distance," Miela suggested finally. "They cannot tell what the hour is. They may be near here now, coming back."

The girls were rested and warmed now, and we started off again with the platform. We flew low over the tree-tops, following the trail as best we could, but in the semi-darkness we could see very little from above. After a time we gave it up and returned to the shore.

Again we waited, now very much alarmed. And then finally we decided to return to the Great City for the night. Anina might have missed us some way, we thought, and flown directly home. She might be there waiting for us when we arrived. If not, we would return again with several hundred girls, and with them scour the country carefully back as near the Lone City as we dared go.

With our hearts heavy with apprehension we started back across the channel. Lua, Mercer and Anina were separated from us. All had been captured, perhaps, by our enemies! Things were, indeed, in a very bad way.

Without unusual incident we sighted the Light Country shore. Three girls were winging their way swiftly toward us.

"They wish to speak with us, Alan," said Miela. "From the Great City they seem to come. Perhaps it is Anina."

Our hopes were soon dispelled, for Anina was not one of them; they were three of the girls we had directed to patrol the seacoast.

When they neared us Miela flew off the platform and joined them. They circled about for a time, flying close together, then Miela left them and returned to me, while they hovered overhead. Her face was clouded with anxiety as she alighted beside me.

"They were near the Water City a short time ago. And they say the light-ray is being used there. They saw it flashing up, and dared not go closer."

The light-ray in the Water City! My heart sunk with dismay. The cylinder I held in my hand I had thought the only one in use in all the Light Country. With it I felt supreme. And now they had it also in the Water City!

One of the girls flung up her hand suddenly and called to Miela.

"See, Alan—a boat!"

I looked down to where Miela pointed. The sea was still rough from the storm, but no longer lashed into fury. Coming toward us, close inshore and from the direction of the Water City, I saw a boat speeding along over the spent waves. And as I looked, a narrow beam of light, green, shading into red, shot up from the boat and hung wavering in the air like a little search-light striving to pierce the gray mist of the sky!

THE THEFT OF THE LIGHT-RAY

The touch of soft, cool hands on his face brought Mercer back to sudden consciousness. He opened his eyes; Anina was sitting beside him, regarding him gravely.

"Wake up, my friend Ollie. Time now to wake up."

He sat up, rubbing his eyes. The same dim twilight obscured everything around. For an instant he was confused.

"Why, I've been asleep." He got to his feet. "Do you think it's been long, Anina? Maybe the men have started off. Let's go see."

Anina had already been to see; she had awakened some little time before and, leaving Mercer asleep, had flown up ahead over the tree-tops.

The men were just then breaking camp, and she had returned to wake up Mercer. They ate their last remaining pieces of bread, drank from the little pool of water, and were soon ready to start on after their quarry.

"How long will it take them to reach the gorge, Anina?"

"Not very long—four times farther reach Lone City."

By which Mercer inferred that within three or four hours, perhaps, they would be at the place where they hoped to turn the men back.

They started off slowly up the trail, Mercer carrying the folded blanket, and Anina wearing the fur jacket. They soon came upon the smoldering fire that marked the other party's night encampment. The men were, Mercer judged, perhaps a mile or so ahead of them.

They continued on, walking slowly, for they did not want to overtake the slow-traveling men ahead. The look of the country, what they could see of it in the darkness, was unchanged. The trail seemed bending steadily to the right, and after a time they came to the bank of a river which the trail followed. It was a broad stream, perhaps a quarter of a mile across, with a considerable current sweeping down to the sea.

They kept to the trail along the river bank for nearly another hour. Then Anina abruptly halted, pulling Mercer partly behind a tree trunk.

"Another fire," she whispered. "They stop again."

They could see the glow of the fire, close by the river bank among the trees. Very cautiously they approached and soon made out the vague outlines of a boat moored to the bank. It seemed similar to the one in which they had come down the bayous from the Great City, only slightly larger.

"Other men," whispered Anina. "From Lone City."

Mercer's heart sank. A party from the Lone City—more of Tao's men to join those he had set free! All his fine plans were swept away. The men would all go up to the Lone City now in the boat, of course. There was nothing he could do to stop them. And now Tao would learn of the failure of his plans.

Mercer's first idea was to give up and return to the shore of the sea; but Anina kept on going cautiously forward, and he followed her.

The fire, they could see as they got closer, was built a little back from the water, with a slight rise of ground between it and the boat. There were some thirty men gathered around; they seemed to be cooking.

"You stand here, Ollie," Anina whispered. "I go hear what they say. Stand very quiet and wait. I come back."

Mercer sat down with his back against a tree and waited. Anina disappeared almost immediately. He heard no sound of her flight, but a moment later he thought he saw her dropping down through the trees just outside the circle of light from the fire. From where he was sitting he could see the boat also; he thought he made out the figure of a man sitting in it, on guard. The situation, as Mercer understood it from what Anina told him when she returned, seemed immeasurably worse even than he had anticipated.

Tao had been making the Water City the basis of his insidious propaganda, rather than the Great City, as we had supposed. He had been in constant communication by boat with his men in the Water City; and now affairs there were ripe for more drastic operations.

This boat Mercer had come upon was intended to be Tao's first armed invasion of the Light Country—some twenty of his most trusted men armed with the light-ray. Joining his emissaries in the Water City, and with the large following among the people there which they had already secured, they planned to seize the government and obtain control of the city. Then, using it as a base, they could spread out for a conquest of the entire nation. Mercer listened with whitening face while Anina told him all this as best she could.

"But—but why does he want to attack the Light Country, Anina? I thought he wanted to go and conquer our earth."

THE FIRE PEOPLE

"Very big task—your earth," the girl answered. "Light Country more easy. Many light -rays in the Great City. Those he needs before he goes to your earth. More simple to get those than make others."

Mercer understood it then. The large quantity of light -ray ammunition stored in the Great City was what Tao was after. This was his way of getting it, and once he had it, and control of the Light Country besides he would be in a much better position to attack the earth.

The idea came to Mercer then to steal the boat and escape with it. If he could do that, the enemies would have to return to the Lone City on foot, and the threatened invasion of the Light Country would thus be postponed for a time at least. Meanwhile, with the boat he could hasten back to me with news of the coming invasion.

These thoughts were running through his head while Anina was talking. It was a daring plan, but it might be done. There was apparently only one man in the boat, and the slight rise of ground between it and the fire made him out of sight, though not out of hearing, of the others.

"Can you run the boat, Anina?"

The girl nodded eagerly. Mercer drew a long breath.

"We'll take a chance. It's the only way. They've got that cursed light -ray." He shivered as he thought of the danger they were about to invite.

Then he explained to Anina what they were to do. She listened carefully, with the same expectant, eager look on her face he had seen there so often before.

They left the blanket and fur jacket on the ground, and, making a wide detour around the fire, came back to the river bank several hundred yards above the boat. They stood at the water's edge, looking about them. The boat was just around a slight bend in the stream; the glimmer of the fire showed plainly among the trees. Intense quiet prevailed; only the murmur of the water flowing past, and occasionally the raised voice of one of the men about the fire, broke the stillness.

Mercer stared searchingly into the girl's eyes as she stood there quietly at his side. She met his gaze steadily.

"You're a wonderful little girl," he whispered to her, and then abruptly added: "Come on. Don't make any splash if you can help it. And remember, if anything goes wrong, never mind me. Fly away—if you can."

They waded slowly into the water. The current carried them rapidly along. Side by side, with slow, careful strokes, they swam, keeping close to shore. The river was shallow—hardly over their heads. The water was cold and, Mercer thought, curiously buoyant.

It seemed hardly more than a moment before the shadowy black figure of outlines of the boat loomed ahead. They could make out the figure of its single occupant, sitting with his arm on the gunwale. They swam hardly at all now, letting the current carry them forward. As silent as two drifting logs they dropped down upon the boat and in another moment were clinging to a bit of rope that chanced to be hanging over its stern.

The bow of the boat was nosed against the bank; it lay diagonally downstream, with its stern some twenty feet from shore. Its occupant was sitting amidships, facing the bow. Mercer drew himself up until his eyes were above the stern of the boat and saw him plainly. He was slouching down as though dozing. His elbow was crooked, carelessly over the gunwale.

Mercer's heart gave an exultant leap as he saw a little cylinder in the man's hand. There was a little projection on the boat at the water line, and, working along this with his hands, Mercer edged slowly toward the man. He knew he could not be heard, for the murmur of the water slipping past the sides of the boat drowned the slight noise he made.

He edged his way along, with not much more than his face out of water, until he was directly beneath the motionless form in the boat.

Mercer's heart was beating so it seemed to smother him. Slowly he pulled himself up until the fingers of his left hand gripped the gunwale hardly more than a foot or two behind the man's back. His other hand reached forward. He must have made a slight noise, for the man sat suddenly upright, listening.

Mercer's right hand shot out. His fingers closed over the little cylinder and the hand holding it. He bent it inward, twisting the man's wrist. His thumb fumbled for the little button Anina had described. There was a tiny puff of light; the man's body wavered, then fell forward inert. Mercer climbed into the boat. He looked back. Anina was pulling herself up over the stern. A long pole lay across the seats. He picked it up and started with it toward the bow. And then he tripped over something and fell headlong, dropping the pole with a clatter.

As he picked himself up there came a shout from the men in the woods. Mercer hurried forward and cast off the rope that held the boat to the bank. It had been tied more or less permanently at this end. As he fumbled at the knots he heard Anina's soft, anxious voice calling: "Hurry, Ollie, hurry!"

THE FIRE PEOPLE

The shouts from the woods continued. The knots loosened finally. The boat slid back away from the bank; with the pole Mercer shoved the bow around. An instant later Anina had started the mechanism, and in a broad curve they swung silently out into the river.

Up from the woods shot a beam of the greenish-red light. It darted to and fro for an instant, almost vertically in the air, and Mercer heard the crackle of the tree-tops as they burst into flame under its heat. Then it swung downward, but before it could reach the water level the rise of ground at the bank cut it off.

Without realizing it, Mercer had been holding his breath as he watched. Now he let it out with a long sigh of relief.

"We did it, Anina—we did it," he said exultantly. "And we've got a light-ray, too."

A moment later they swept around a bend in the river, out of sight and out of hearing of their enemies.

THE STORM

On the little stern seat of the boat Mercer and Anina sat side by side, the girl steering by a small tiller that lay between them. They were well out in the middle of the river now, speeding silently along with its swift current. They made extraordinary speed. Both banks of the river were visible in the twilight—dim, wooded hills stretching back into darkness.

The stream widened steadily as they advanced, until near, its mouth it had become a broad estuary. They followed its right shore now and soon were out in the Narrow Sea.

"We'd better go right on across," said Mercer. "It's too early for Alan to be at the end of the trail. He won't be there till to -night. We can reach the Great City before he starts."

They decided to do that, and headed straight out into the sea. They had been cold, sitting there in the wind, and wet to the skin. But the boat contained several furry jackets, which the men had left in it, and in the bottom, near the stern, a cubical metal box which lighted up like an electric radiator. By this they had dried and warmed themselves, and now, each with a fur jacket on, they felt thoroughly comfortable.

Mercer was elated at what they had accomplished. He could see now how fortunate a circumstance it was that we had set the men free. He would not have stumbled upon this other party, and the invasion of the Light Country would have begun, had we not released them.

He talked enthusiastically about what we were to do next, and Anina listened, saying very little, but following his words with eager attention. Once he thought she was more interested in the words themselves than in what he was saying, and said so.

"Your language—so very easy it is. I want to learn it soon if I can."

"Why, you know it already," he protested. "And how the deuce you ever got it so quickly beats me."

She smiled.

"When you say words—very easy then for me to remember. Not many words in spoken language."

He shook his head.

"Well, however you do it, the result's all right. I'm mighty glad, too. Why, when I get you back home on earth—" He stopped in sudden confusion.

She put her hand on his arm.

"Miela says your earth is very wonderful. Tell me about it."

She listened to his glowing words. "And opera—what is that?" she asked once when he paused.

He described the Metropolitan Opera House, and the newer, finer one in Boston. She listened to his description of the music with flushed face and shining eyes.

"How beautiful—that music! Can you sing, Ollie?"

"No," he admitted, "but I can play a little on a guitar. I wish I had one here."

"I can sing," said the girl: "Miela says I can sing very well."

He leaned toward her, brushing the blue feathers of her wing lightly with his hand.

"Sing for me," he said softly. "I'll bet you sing beautifully."

It may have been their situation, or what they had been through together, or the girl's nearness to him now with her long braids of golden hair, the graceful sweep of her blue-feathered wings that matched the blue of her eyes, her red lips parted in song—but whatever it was, Mercer thought he had never heard so sweet a voice. She sang a weird little song. It was in a minor key, with curious cadences that died away and ended nowhere—the folk song of a different race, a different planet, yet vibrant with the ever unsatisfied longing of the human soul.

She sang softly, staring straight before her, without thought of her singing, thinking only of her song. She ended with a tender phrase that might have been a sigh—a quivering little half sob that died away in her throat and left the song unfinished. Her hands were folded quiet in her lap; her eyes gazed out on the gray waste of water about the boat.

Mercer breathed again.

"That is beautiful, Anina. What is it?"

She turned to him and smiled.

"Just love song. You like it, my friend Ollie?"

"It's wonderful. But it's—it's so sad—and—and sort of weird isn't it?"

"That is love, my mother says. Love is sad."

Mercer's heart was beating fast.

"Is it always sad, Anina? I don't think so—do you?"

There was no trace of coquetry in her eyes; she sighed tremulously.

"I do not know about love. But what I feel here"—she put her hand on her breast—"I do not understand, Ollie. And when I sing—they are very sad and sweet, the thoughts of music, and they say things to the heart that the brain does not understand. Is it that way with you?"

Unnoticed by the two, a storm cloud had swept up over the horizon behind them, and the sky overhead was blotted now with its black. They had not seen it nor heeded the distant flashing of lightning. A sudden thunderclap startled them now into consciousness of the scene about them. The wind rushed on them from behind. The sea was rising rapidly; the boat scudded before it.

"A storm! Look at it, Anina, behind us!"

There was nothing in sight now but the gray sea, broken into waves that were beginning to curl, white and angry. Behind them the darkness was split with jagged forks of lightning. The thunder rolled heavily and ominously in the distance, with occasional sharp cracks near at hand.

"Look, Anina—there comes the rain! See it there behind us! I hope it won't be a bad storm. I wouldn't want to be out in this little tub."

The wind veered to the left, increasing steadily. The sea was lashed into foam; its spray swept over the boat, drenching them thoroughly.

The waves, turning now with the wind, struck the boat on its stern quarter. One curled aboard, sloshing an inch or two of water about the bottom of the boat. Mercer feared it would interfere with the mechanism, but Anina reassured him.

As the waves increased in size, Mercer swung the boat around so as to run directly before them. The stern frequently was lifted clear of the water now, the boat losing headway as a great cloud of hissing steam arose from behind.

After a time the Light Country shore came into sight. They were close upon it before they saw it through the rain and murk. They seemed to be heading diagonally toward it.

"Where are we, Anina?" Mercer asked anxiously.

The girl shook her head.

Steadily they were swept inward. The shore line, as they drew closer, was to Mercer quite unfamiliar. There were no bayous here, no inundated land. Instead, a bleak line of cliffs fronted them—a perpendicular wall against which the waves beat furiously. They could see only a short distance. The line of cliffs extended ahead of them out of sight in the gray of the sheets of rain.

THE FIRE PEOPLE

They were slanting toward the cliffs, and Mercer knew if he did not do something they would be driven against them in a few moments more.

"We'll have to turn out, Anina. We can't land along here. We must keep away if we can."

With the waves striking its stern quarter again, the boat made much heavier weather. It seemed to Mercer incredible that it should stay afloat. He found himself thoroughly frightened now, but when he remembered that Anina was in no danger he felt relieved. He had made her lie down in the boat, where she would be more sheltered from the wind and rain. Now he hastily bade her get up and sit beside him.

"We might be swamped any minute, Anina. You sit there where you won't get caught if we go over."

They swept onward, Mercer keeping the boat offshore as best he could.

"Haven't you any idea where we are, Anina? How far along do these cliffs extend?"

A huge, jagged pinnacle of rock, like a great cathedral spire set in the cliff, loomed into view ahead. Anina's face brightened, when she saw it.

"The way to the Water City," she cried. "A river there is—ahead. Not so very far now."

In spite of all Mercer could do, they were blowing steadily closer to the wave - lashed cliffs.

He began to despair. "If anything happens, Anina—you fly up at once. You hear? Don't you wait. You can't help me any. I'll make out some way. You say good -by to Alan and your mother and sister for me—if—" He fell silent a moment, then said softly: "And, Anina, if that should happen, I want you to know that I think you're the sweetest, most wonderful little girl I ever met. And, Anina dear—"

The girl gripped his arm with a cry of joy.

"See, Ollie! There, ahead, the cliffs end. That is the Water City river! See it there?"

The mouth of a broad estuary, with the waves rolling up into it, came swiftly into view. They rounded the rocky headland and entered it, running now almost directly before the wind. The river narrowed after a short distance to a stream very much like the one they had left in the Twilight Country.

Mercer turned to the quiet little girl beside him.

"Well, Anina, we've certainly had some trip. I wouldn't want to go through it again."

Mercer thought the situation over. They could stay where they were in the river for an hour or two until the storm was entirely over, and then go back to the Great City. On the other hand, now that they were here, Mercer felt a great curiosity to see this other city where Tao's men had created trouble. Why should they not use these few hours of waiting to see it?

"We might get a line on how things stand up there to tell Alan when we get back," Mercer said when he explained his ideas to Anina. "It won't take long." Very probably it was the light-ray cylinder in his hand which influenced his decision, for he added: "We can't get into any trouble, you know; there's no light-ray here yet."

And so they went on.

There was a perceptible current coming down the river. The water was cold and clear, and in the brighter light now he could see down into it in many places to the bottom, six or eight feet below. The region seemed utterly uninhabited; no sign of a house or even a boat on the river met them as they advanced.

"Mightn't there be boats along here?" Mercer asked once. "How far up is this place?"

"Not far now—beyond there."

The river appeared to terminate abruptly up ahead against the side of a frowning brown cliff, but Mercer saw a moment later that it opened out around a bend to the left.

"Around that next bend?"

She nodded.

It seemed incredible to Mercer that the second largest city in Mercury lay hidden in the midst of this desolation.

"We'll meet boats," he said. "What will the people think of me? Don't let's start anything if we can help it."

"You lie there." Anina indicated the bottom of the boat at her feet. "No one see you then. I steer. They do not notice me. Nobody care who I am."

Mercer had still the very vaguest of ideas as to what they would do when they got to the Water City. As a matter of fact, he really was more curious just to see it than anything else. But there was another reason that urged him on. Both he and Anina were hungry.

THE FIRE PEOPLE

They had eaten very little since leaving the Great City the night before; and now that it was again evening, they were famished. They had rummaged the boat thoroughly, but evidently the men had taken all their supplies ashore with them, for nothing was in the boat.

"We'll have to dope out some way to get something to eat," said Mercer.

They came upon the sharp bend in the river Anina had indicated. Following close against one rocky shore, they swept around the bend, and the Water City lay spread out before Mercer's astonished eyes.

THE WATER CITY

It had stopped raining; the sky overhead was luminous with diffused sunlight; the scene that lay before Mercer was plainly visible. The river had opened abruptly into a broad, shallow, nearly circular lake, some five or six miles across. The country here showed an extraordinary change from that they had passed through. The lake appeared to occupy a depression in the surrounding hills, like the bottom of a huge, shallow bowl. From the water's edge on all sides the ground sloped upward. It was no longer a barren, rocky land, but seemingly covered with a rich heavy soil, dotted with tropical trees. That it was under a high state of cultivation was evident. Mercer saw tier upon tier of rice terraces on the hillsides.

But what astonished him most was the city itself. It covered almost the entire surface of the lake—a huge collection of little palm -thatched shacks built upon platforms raised above the water on stilts. Some of the houses were larger and built of stone, with their foundations in the water.

Off to one side were two or three little islands, an acre or less in extent, fringed with palms and coconut trees. In nearly the center of the lake stood a stone castle, two stories in height, with minarets ornamenting its corners. An open stretch of water surrounded it.

There was little of regularity about this extraordinary city, and no evidence of streets, for the houses were set down quite haphazard wherever open space afforded. In some places they were more crowded together than others, although seldom closer than twenty or thirty feet.

Around the larger ones there was a little more open water, as though the owners controlled it and forbade building there. Some of the smaller houses were connected by little wooden bridges. Anina said this was where two or more families of relatives had located together.

There were a few boats moving about—little punts hollowed out of logs and propelled by long poles—and Mercer saw many others, some of them larger like the one he and Anina were in, tied up by the houses. It was now the time of the evening meal. The workers had returned from the terraces; there were few moving about the city. Occasionally a girl would dart up from one of the houses and wing her way to another, but beyond that there were no signs of activity.

Anina took command of the boat now, slowing it down and heading for the nearest of the houses, which were hardly more than quarter of a mile away. Mercer stretched himself out in the bottom of the boat, covering himself with a large piece of fabric that lay there. He felt that he would be unnoticed, even should a girl chance to pass directly overhead. But he could see nothing of the city from where he was, and soon grew restless and anxious to do something else.

"I'm coming up, Anina," he said once. "Shucks! Nobody can do anything to us. Haven't I got this light-ray?"

But Anina was obdurate, and made him stay where he was.

They went slowly forward and were soon among the houses. On the front platform of one a man sat fishing. A little naked boy slid down into the water from another, swimming as though born to the water. Both stared at Anina curiously as she passed slowly by, but they said nothing. A girl looked out of the window of another house and waved her hand in friendly greeting, which Anina answered.

Mercer, lying with all but his face covered by the cloth, could see only the sides of the boat, the bottom of the cross-seat over his head, and Anina as she sat above him in the stern.

"Where do you suppose the Tao people hang out around here?" he suddenly asked. "If we could—"

The girl silenced him with a gesture.

He lowered his voice. "Try and find out where they are, Anina," he whispered.

Anina steered the boat directly under several of the houses, which must have been quite a usual proceeding, for it attracted no attention. A girl flew close to them once, and Anina called to her. The girl alighted on the stern of the boat for a moment; Mercer slid the cloth over his face and held himself motionless. Then he heard Anina's voice calling to him softly. He slid the cloth back; the girl had gone.

"She says Tao's men live, there—large house, of wood," said Anina, pointing off to one side.

Mercer nearly rapped his head against the seat above him in his excitement.

"You know which house? Let's go there. Maybe we can hear what they're saying. Can we get under it?"

She nodded.

"Let's try, Anina," he said eagerly. "You steer us slow right under it, just as if you were going past. If there's nobody in sight you can stop underneath, can't you? Maybe we can hear what they're saying."

"I try," the girl said simply.

"I'll lay still," encouraged Mercer. "Nobody will bother about you. Just sneak in and see what happens. If anybody sees you, keep going."

He was all excitement, and in spite of Anina's protests wriggled about continually, trying to see where they were.

The house that the girl had pointed out lay only a few hundred yards ahead. It was one of the largest of the wooden buildings—sixty or seventy feet long at least—single story, with a high sloping thatched roof.

It was raised on a platform some six feet above the water, which, in front, had a little flight of wooden steps leading down to the surface. There was a hundred feet of open water on all sides of the building. The boat, moving slowly, slipped through the water almost without a sound.

"Where are we now?" Mercer whispered impatiently. "Aren't we there yet?"

The girl put a finger to her lips. "Almost there. Quiet now."

She steered straight for the house. There was no one in sight, either about the house itself or about those in its immediate vicinity. A moment more and the boat slid beneath the building into semi -darkness.

Anina shut the power off and stood up. The floor of the house was just above her head. In front of her, near the center of the building, she saw the side walls of an inner inclosure some twenty feet square. These walls came down to the surface, making a room like a basement to the dwelling. A broad doorway, with a sliding door that now stood open, gave ingress.

The boat had now almost lost headway. Anina nosed its bow into this doorway, and grasping one of the pilings near at hand, brought it to rest.

Mercer, at a signal from her, climbed cautiously to his feet, still holding the little light -ray cylinder in his hand.

"What's that in there?" he whispered.

Beyond the doorway, through which the bow of the boat projected, there was complete darkness.

"Lower room," Anina whispered back. "Store things in there. And boat landing, too."

"Let's go in and see."

Mercer started toward the bow of the boat. Six feet or more of it was inside the doorway. He made his way carefully into the bow, and found himself inside the basement of the house.

THE FIRE PEOPLE

In the dimness of this interior he could just make out the outlines of things around. The doorway was located at a corner of the inclosure. In front lay a small open space of water. At one side a platform about two feet above the surface formed the floor of the room. A tiny punt lay moored to it. Farther back a small, steep flight of steps led up through a rectangular opening to the building above.

Most of the light in this lower room came down through this opening; and now, as Mercer stood quiet looking about him, he could hear plainly the voices of men in the room above.

Anina was beside him.

"They're up there," he whispered, pointing. "Let's land and see if we can get up those stairs a ways and hear what they're saying."

They stood a moment, undecided, and then from the silence and darkness about them they distinctly heard a low muffled sound.

"What's that?" whispered Mercer, startled. "Didn't you hear that, Anina? There's something over there by the bottom of the steps."

They listened, but only the murmur of the voices from above, and an occasional footstep, broke the stillness.

"I tell you I heard something," Mercer persisted. "There's something over there." He rattled a bit of rope incautiously, as if to startle a rat from its hiding place. "Let's tie up, Anina."

They made the boat fast, but in such a way that they could cast it loose quickly.

"We might want to get out of here in a hurry," Mercer whispered with a grin. "You never can tell, Anina."

He stood stock still. The sound near at hand was repeated. It was unmistakable this time—a low, stifled moan.

Mercer stepped lightly out of the boat onto the platform. A few boxes, a coil of rope, and other odds and ends stood about. He felt his way forward among them toward the bottom of the steps. He heard the moan again, and now he saw the outlines of a human figure lying against the farther wall.

Anina was close behind him.

"There's somebody over there," he whispered. "Hurt or sick, maybe."

They crept forward.

It was a woman, bound hand and foot and gagged. Mercer bent over and tore the cloth from her face. In another instant Anina was upon her knees, sobbing softly, with her mother's head in her lap.

They loosed the cords that held her, and chaffed her stiffened limbs. She soon recovered, for she was not injured. She told Anina her story then—how Baar had captured her in her home while she was waiting for Miela and me, and how two of his men had brought her here to the Water City by boat at once.

That was all she knew, except that this house was the headquarters of Tao's emissaries, who, it appeared, were now allied with Baar and his party.

Anina whispered all this to Mercer when her mother had finished.

"Let's get out of here," said Mercer.

The responsibility of two women, especially the elder Lua, who could not fly, weighed suddenly upon him, and his first thought was to get back to the Great City at once.

Anina helped her mother into the boat.

"Wait," she whispered to Mercer. "I hear what they say. You wait here."

She went to the foot of the steps and began climbing them cautiously.

"Not on your life, I won't wait here," Mercer muttered to himself, and, gripping the light-ray cylinder firmly as though he feared it might get away from him, he joined Anina on the stairway.

Slowly, cautiously they made their way upward. The steps were fairly wide, and they went up almost side by side. From near the top they could see a portion of the room above.

The corner of a table showed, around which a number of men were gathered, eating. A woman was moving about the room serving them.

Their words, from here, were plainly audible. Mercer would have gone a step or two higher, without thought of discovery, but Anina held him back. "Wait, Ollie. I hear now what they say."

They stood silent. The men were talking earnestly. Mercer could hear their words, but of course understood nothing he heard.

"What do they say, Anina?" he whispered impatiently after a moment.

"Baar is here with two or three of his men. He talks with Tao's men. They talk about men from Twilight Country. Waiting for them now. Speak of storm. Worried—because men do not come. Waiting for light-ray."

"They'll have a long wait," Mercer chuckled. "Let's get out of here, Anina."

He must have made a slight noise, or perhaps he and Anina, crouching there on the stairs, were seen by some one above. He never knew quite how it occurred, but, without warning, a man stood at the opening, looking down at them.

There was a shout, and the room above was in instant turmoil. Mercer lost his head. Anina pulled at him and said something, but he did not hear her. He only knew that they had been discovered, and that most of their enemies in the Water City were crowded together in this one room at hand. And he had the light - ray—the only one in the city.

A sudden madness possessed him. He tore away from Anina and, climbing up the steps of the stairway, leaped into the room above.

Twenty or thirty men faced him, most of them about the table. Several had started hastily to their feet; two or three chairs were overturned.

The man who had been looking down into the opening darted back as Mercer came up, and shouted again.

Mercer saw it was Baar.

THE WATER CITY.

The men around the table were now all on their feet. One of them picked up a huge metal goblet and flung it at Mercer's head. The last remaining bit of reason Mercer had left fled from him. Without thought of what he was about, he raised the metal cylinder; his thumb found the little button and pressed it hard; he waved the cylinder back and forth before him.

It was over in an instant. Mercer relaxed his pressure on the button and staggered back. He was sick and faint from what he had seen—with the realization of what he had done. Flames were rising all about him. The room was full of smoke. He held his breath, finding his way back somehow to the stairway, with the agonized screams of the men ringing in his ears. He caught a glimpse of Anina's white face as she stood there where he had left her.

"Good God. Anina! Go back! Go back! I'm coming!"

He tripped near the top of the stairs and fell in a heap onto the platform below, but he still held the cylinder clutched tightly in his hand.

Anina groped her way down to him. He gripped her by the arm. He was trembling like a leaf. The crackling of the burning house above came down to him; the cries of the men were stilled.

"Come, Anina," he half whispered. "Hurry—let's get away, anywhere. Home—out of this cursed city."

Lua was still in the boat. Her calm, steady glance brought Mercer back to his senses. They shoved the boat out from under the house, and in a moment more were heading back through the city. The building they had left was now a mass of flames, with a great cloud of smoke, rolling up from it. A woman stood on the front platform an instant, and then, screaming, flung herself into the water.

The city was in commotion. Faces appeared at windows; girls flew up and gathered in a frightened flock, circling about the burning building; boats miraculously appeared from everywhere. Lua was steering their boat on its tortuous way between the houses. She put the boat nearly to full speed, and as they swept past a house nearly collided with a punt that was crossing behind it.

Mercer's nerves were still shaken. He handed Anina the light-ray cylinder.

"Here—take it, Anina. I don't want the cursed thing. Shoot it up into the air. Somebody might try and stop us. That'll scare them. Careful you don't hit anything!"

Anina played the light about in the air for a time, but soon there were so many girls flying about she had to shut it off. A few minutes more and they had passed the last of the houses, swept around the bend in the river, and left the frightened city out of sight behind them.

They had left the river and, following close along shore, headed for the bayous that led up to the Great City. The storm had now entirely passed, leaving the daylight unusually bright and a fresh coolness in the air. The sea was still rough, although not alarmingly so, and the boat made comparatively slow progress. It was two hours or more—to Mercer it seemed a whole day—before they were nearing the bayous. Anina was sitting by his side in the center of the boat. Lua was steering.

"You hungry, Ollie?" the girl asked, smiling.

Mercer shook his head. He had forgotten they had intended to eat in the Water City.

"I very hungry. Soon we—"

She stopped abruptly, staring up into the sky ahead of them.

Mercer followed her glance. A little black blob showed against the gray; off to one side two other smaller black dots appeared.

"What's that?" cried Mercer, alarmed.

They watched a few moments in silence. Then Mercer took the cylinder, and flashed its light into the air.

"If it's anybody connected with Tao, that'll show they'd better keep away," he explained grimly.

Anina smiled. "Tao people cannot fly, Ollie."

A few moments more and they saw what it was. And within ten minutes they had landed at the mouth of one of the bayous, and Miela and I were with them.

PREPARATIONS FOR WAR

The months that followed were the busiest, I think, of my life. I began by a complete reorganization of this government of which I found myself the head. For the doddering old councilors of the late king I substituted men whom I selected from among those of the city's prominent business men who cared to serve.

The personnel of the police force I allowed to remain, for I soon saw they were inclined to act very differently under me than under my predecessor. The various other officials of this somewhat vague organization I subjected to a thorough weeding out.

The net result was chaos for a time, but, far more quickly than I had anticipated, I had things running again. I made no radical changes except in personnel. I attempted to do nothing that was outside the then existing laws, and no new laws were passed. But from the very first I made it clear that I was not one to be trifled with.

Within a few days after I was put into power I interviewed Fuero and his scientific confrères. I found them a body of grave men who represented the highest type of the nation. They made it plain to me at once that they would not concern themselves in any way with government affairs. Two years before they had recognized Tao's menace, and had been preparing for it by the manufacture of large quantities of war material which, in case of extreme necessity, they would turn over to the government. This armament, as Miela had told me, they guarded themselves, not trusting it even to their workmen.

The scientific men, I understood now, were among the richest in the nation, owing to the widespread use of their industrial appliances. It was only a portion of this wealth that they were expending in the manufacture of armament.

I demanded the release to me of this war material. I explained them my plans, and told them in detail of Tao's visit to earth. They held several conferences over a period of two or three days, but in the end I got what I asked for.

So much for affairs in the Great City. I recognized during these days the possibility of an armed invasion from the Twilight Country. I was better prepared to meet it now, should it come, and I at once took steps to be warned as far in advance as possible. To this end I had girls patrolling the Narrow Sea, not only on our shore, but over in the Twilight Country as well; and I was satisfied that if Tao made any move we would be notified at once. Simultaneously with all this, we devoted ourselves to the unification of the nation, for in very truth it seemed about to disintegrate. Here it was that the girls were of the greatest assistance.

We organized them into an army which consisted of fifty squads of ten girls each, with a leader for each squad. All of these girls were armed with the light-ray cylinders. With this "flying army" Mercer and I made a tour of the Light Country cities. We wasted no time with formalities, but rounded up Tao's men wherever we could find them, and transported them unceremoniously back to the Twilight Country shore.

In two or three of the cities—the Water City particularly—there was a show of rebellion among the people; but our light-rays cowed them instantly, and in no instance did we have to kill or injure any one. Through Miela I made speeches everywhere. It was not my wish to hold the country in sullen subjection, and to that end I appealed to their patriotism in this coming war against Tao and the Twilight People. This aspect of the matter met with ready response, and everywhere our meetings ended in enthusiastic acclaim.

We started now to raise an army of young men, which we proposed to transport across the Narrow Sea for land operations in the Twilight Country. Before a week had passed I saw, by the response that came from my various proclamations, that conscription would be unnecessary. With this tangible evidence of the coming war the patriotism of the people grew by leaps and bounds. The fact that the girls of the Great City were not only in favor of it, but were actually already in service—a thing unprecedented in the history of the nation—brought the sympathies of all the women with us strongly.

Through the governors of each city I raised a separate army of young men, officered by the older men, most of whom had taken part in past fighting. Each of these little armies, as yet without arms, was drilled and held in readiness for orders from the Great City.

I had, during all this time, selected as many able men as possible from among the Great City's population, and given them over to Fuero and his associates for training in the use of the light-ray rockets, the larger projectors, protective measures against the ray, and many other appliances which I understood only vaguely myself.

It was after our return from the tour of the different cities, and before the recruiting of the young men was fairly under way, when like a bombshell came the news from our flying patrol that a fleet of armed boats was coming down the river from the Lone City. The attack from Tao was at hand, and our preparations were still far from complete. We had our army of girls in active operation, and that was all. Tao's boats would reach the Light Country shore in a few hours. There was no time for anything but the hastiest of preparations. We decided then to call the army of girls and meet the boats in the Narrow Sea, turning them back if possible.

I have now to explain the method of defense against the light -ray. In theory I only vaguely understood it. In practice it was simple and, like most defenses, only partially effective.

Bob Trevor, has already mentioned it—the suits of black cloth he saw in the Mercutian camp in Wyoming. It was not, as he had afterward supposed, a dye for fabrics. Instead, it was the thread of a worm—like our silk worm—which in its natural state was black and was impervious to the ray. By that I mean a substance whose molecules increased their vibration rate only slightly from a brief contact with the ray.

It was only partly efficacious, for after an exposure of a minute or more the intense heat of the ray was communicated. It then became partly penetrable, and anything close behind it would be destroyed.

We had under manufacture at this time a number of protective devices by which this substance might be used. Boats had, in the past, been equipped with a sort of shield or hood in front, making them more or less impervious to a direct horizontal beam of the light.

Tao's boats which now threatened us were so protected, I was informed by the girls who reported them. Recognizing the probability of an attack by us from the air, they also had a covering of the cloth, like a canopy above them. But as may be readily understood, such protection could be made only partly effective.

I had already manufactured, at Miela's suggestion, a number of shields for our girls to carry while in flight. These consisted of the fabric in very light, almost diaphanous, form, hung upon a flexible frame of very thin strips of bamboo. It was some twelve feet broad across the top, narrowing rapidly into a long fluttering tail like a kite.

There was nothing rigid about this shield. Its two or three bamboo ribs were as flexible as a whip, with the veiling—it was hardly more than that—fluttering below them almost entirely unsupported. In weight, the whole approximated one -twelfth that of a girl, not at all a difficult amount to carry.

Within two hours after the report came—it was near midday—we were ready to start from the Great City to repel Tao's attack. Our forces consisted of some six hundred girls, each armed with a light -ray cylinder and a shield. This was the organization I have already mentioned, fifty squads of ten, each with a leader; and fifty other girls, the most daring and expert in the air, who were to act independently.

We had two platforms, protected by the fabric, and with a sort of canopy around the sides underneath, over which the girls grasping the handles could fly. Mercer and Anina rode on one platform, and Miela and I on the other. All of us were dressed in the black garments.

On each of the platforms we had mounted a projector of higher power than the hand cylinders, although of course of much less effective range than those the Mercutians had used in Wyoming.

Thus equipped we rose into the air from the castle grounds in the Great City, with a silent, awed multitude watching us—as strange an army, probably, as ever went forth to battle.

THE BATTLE

We swept out over the Great City, flying in the battle -formation we had used many times before on our trips about the country. Mercer's platform and mine were some fifty feet apart, leading. Behind us, in a great semicircle, the girls spread out, fifty little groups of ten, each with its single leader in front. Below, a hundred feet perhaps, the fifty other girls darted back and forth, keeping pace with us. The aspect of these girls, flying thus to battle, was truly extraordinary. The pink -white flesh of their bodies; their limbs incased in the black veiling; their long black or golden hair; and the vivid red or blue feathered wings flashing behind those wide, fluttering, flimsy black shields—it was a sight the like of which I never shall see again.

There was almost no wind, for which I was thankful, as it made our maneuvers in the air considerably less difficult. When we reached the Narrow Sea our patrols reported that Tao's ships were still in the river, waiting for others from the Lone City to join them. We hastened on, for I wished to meet them as near the Twilight shore as possible.

We believed, from the reports our girls had brought us, that the enemy would have some twenty or thirty boats, most of them similar to that in which Mercer and Anina weathered the storm on the way to the Water City.

We assumed that the men in the boats would be armed with the hand light -ray cylinders. These projected a beam not over four inches broad and had an effective range of about five hundred feet. The boats probably would carry large projectors also. They might be set up in the boats ready for use, or they might not.

What range they would have we could not estimate, though we hoped we should encounter nothing more powerful than this one Miela and I had on the platform. Its beam was about twenty inches wide, its effective radius something like a thousand feet.

We did not expect to encounter the very large projectors. We had some in the Great City with a range of something like ten miles, and others of lesser range that spread the ray out fan shape. But these were extremely heavy, and we were confident it would not be practical to mount them in the boats.

We sighted the enemy in the Narrow Sea just before the Twilight shore was reached. The first intimation we had was the sight of one of the narrow beams of red -green light flashing about in the twilight. As we crept closer, at an altitude of some two thousand feet, we saw the dim outlines of the boats in the water below.

RAY CUMMINGS

There were, I made out, some ten or fifteen in sight. They were heading out into the sea in single file. Miela and I had carefully discussed the tactics we were to employ. Mercer understood our plans, and we had three or four girls detailed to fly close to the platforms and carry our orders about to the leaders of the various little squads.

We sighted the boats when we were about a mile away, and, as I have said, at an altitude of some two thousand feet. They must have seen us soon afterward, for many light -rays now began flashing up from them.

So far as I could determine, each boat seemed armed only with one mounted projector; these I believed to be of somewhat similar power to our own. Our first move was to poise directly over the enemy, rising to an altitude of twenty -five hundred feet. The boats kept straight on their way, and we followed them, circling overhead in lengthening spirals, but keeping well out of range.

I had ordered that none of the rays be flashed at this time, and it must have been difficult for the men in the boats below to see us in the dusk, shrouded as we were in black. They sent up a rocket once; it mounted above us in a slow flaming arc, hung poised an instant, and then descended, plunging into the sea a mile or so away. We heard distinctly the hiss of its contact with the water, and saw, like a quickly dissipating mist, the cloud of steam that arose.

We were not armed with these rockets, for to discharge them from the platforms would have been impractical. But we did not fear them being used against us. Even if true aim had been possible, we could easily avoid their slow flight.

The protecting canopy below the sides of our platform made it difficult to see what was going on below us. Miela and I lay prone, with our heads projecting over its forward end. In this position we had an unobstructed, though somewhat limited, view. The girls carrying us could see nothing. They were guided by watching the other girls flying near them, and by Miela's constant directions.

For some ten or fifteen minutes we circled about over the leading boat. The Twilight shore was now almost over the horizon. The boats showed as little black patches on the gray -black of the sea, but the lights flashing up from them were plainly visible.

The boat that led the line was quite perceptibly drawing away from the others. Already it was a thousand feet or more ahead of the nearest one following. We waited through another period. This leading boat was now beyond range of the others, and, being isolated, I decided to attack it.

151

THE FIRE PEOPLE

"Miela," I said, "tell them all to maintain this level. You and I will go down at that first boat. Have them all remain up here. Tell Mercer if anything goes wrong with us to act as he thinks best."

We waited while these commands were circulated about. Mercer's platform swept close over us, and he shouted: "We won't stay up here."

I persuaded him finally, and then we directed our girls to circle slowly downward with our platform. I ordered a slow descent, for I was in no mind to rush blindly into range of their ray.

We drooped down in a spiral, until at about fifteen hundred feet I ordered the girls to descend no farther. So far as I could make out now, this boat was protected from above by a broad overhanging canopy. Its sides evidently were open, or nearly so, for we could see now the smaller rays flashing out horizontally.

The large projector was mounted in the bow beyond the canopy. Its beam obviously could be directed into the air, for it was now swinging up toward us. But in the horizontal position its range was limited to an arc in front of the boat. I saw then that our play was to attack from a low level, since only in that way could we expect to reach a vulnerable spot in the boat's armor. And I believed that if we could keep behind it they could not reach us with their larger projector.

We swooped downward almost to the water level, and reached it a thousand feet perhaps off to one side of the boat and partly behind it. The smaller projectors flashed out at us, but we were beyond their range. The projector in the bow swung back and forth, and as we skimmed the surface of the water, heading toward the boat, it turned to face us.

What followed happened so quickly I had no time to consult with Miela. She directed our flight. I turned the current into our projector and tried to bring its beam to bear on the boat. We approached within some eight hundred feet of it, darting back and forth, sometimes rising a hundred feet or more, sometimes skimming the surface, but always keeping behind the boat as it turned in an endeavor to face us.

My light -ray beam hit the water frequently, with a great boiling and hissing, sending up clouds of steam that for a moment obscured the scene. Once or twice our opponent's beam flashed over us, but we were beyond its arc before they could bring it directly to bear.

I grew confused at the rapid turns we made. The dark outlines of the boat, with its twenty or thirty flashing red and green lights, seemed everywhere at once. I swung my projector about as best I could, but the swiftly shifting target seemed too elusive. Once, as we dropped suddenly downward, I thought we should plunge into the hissing, roaring water below. Again, the opposing ray swung directly under us, as we darted upward to avoid it.

"I can't make it, Miela," I said. "Hold steady toward them if you can."

She did not answer, but kept her face over the platform's end and issued her swift directions to the girls. Once, as we tilted sharply upward, I caught a glimpse of a black-shape sweeping past, overhead. It was Mercer's platform, flying unswervingly toward the boat, its red-green beam steady before it like a locomotive headlight. We turned to follow; my own light swung dangerously near Mercer, and I turned the current off hastily.

The wind of our forward flight whistled past my ears; Miela's directions to the girls rose shrill above it. I caught a glimpse of the darting lights of the boat ahead. Then, when we were hardly more than six hundred feet away, Mercer's light picked it up. I saw the little lurid red circle it made as it struck the boat's canopy top, and roved along it end to end. Mercer's platform darted lower, and from that angle his light swept under the canopy. A man's scream of agony came to us across the water. The lights on the boat were extinguished; only the yellow glare of the flames rising from its interior fittings remained.

Then, a moment later, the boat's stern rose into the air, and it slid hissing into the water, leaving only a little wreckage and a few struggling forms on the swirling surface.

We swung sharply upward. Again Mercer's platform—its light now extinguished—swept directly over us. His exultant voice floated down.

"We did it, Alan! We did it! Come on up!"

We rose to the upper air, where the girls were still circling about. The other boats were keeping on their course, spreading farther apart now to be out of range of each other's projectors. I had hoped they would turn back with this catastrophe to their leader, but they did not.

I consulted hastily with Miela, and then we gave the order for a general attack, allowing each of the leading girls to act as she saw fit.

Like a great flock of birds we swooped downward upon our prey, spreading out to attack all the boats at once. The girls now turned on their hand lights—a myriad tiny beams darting about in the semi-darkness.

THE FIRE PEOPLE

I cannot attempt to describe the scene that followed. It can be imagined, perhaps, but not told in words. As we swept within range of the lights that swung up from below to meet us, I saw a girl, flying alone, pass directly through one of the red beams. It seemed to strike her sidewise. In an instant she had passed beyond it. I saw the dim outlines of her form as she fluttered onward, wavering and aimless like a wounded bird. And then she fell, turning over and over as with one wing she strove vainly to support herself, until at last, wrapped in the sable shroud of her shield, she plunged with a great splash into the sea.

The flashing light -rays all about us now seemed mingled in inextricable confusion. The girls must have passed through them frequently, protected by their shields; and I know our platform was several times struck by them from below. The absence of sound was uncanny. Only the whistling wind of our flight, the flapping of the girl's wings, and the hissing of steam as our rays struck the water, accompanied this inferno of light.

We swept beyond the boat we had singled out, passing five or six hundred feet above it, and in the effort to avoid its ray turning so that I was unable to bring mine upon it. As we rose again, beyond it, I saw a boat off to the left in flames. A dozen girls had rushed upon it, darting in among its smaller rays to where their own would be effective. But there was only one girl above it now, struggling brokenly to maintain herself in flight. The boat sank with the roar of an explosion of some kind, but in the sudden darkness about I could still see this lone wounded girl fluttering onward.

We were not far away; I pointed her out to Miela, and instead of swinging back we kept on toward her. We contrived to pass close under her, and she fell abruptly almost into my arms. I stretched her out gently on the platform and turned back to Miela, who was kneeling behind our projector.

We were now nearly half a mile from the nearest of the boats. Several of them evidently had been sunk, and two or three others were sinking. One I could make out heading back for the Twilight shore; above it the lights of our girls following showed vivid against the dark -gray sky. Where Mercer's platform was I could not tell.

Miela gripped my shoulder.

"See, Alan—there!" She pointed off to one side. "One of the boats tries to escape."

We were now some five hundred feet above the water. Half a mile beyond us, all its lights out, one of the boats was scurrying away, on across toward the Light Country. For some reason none of our girls seemed following it.

Miela issued a sharp command; we swooped downward at lightning speed and, barely skimming the surface, flew after this escaping enemy. Whether its larger projector had been rendered inoperative, or many of its crew killed, or whether it thought merely to escape us and make a landing in the Light Country, I did not know.

Whatever the reason, no lights showed from this boat as we drew after it. I had our own light out. When we came close within range I flashed it on suddenly. We were flying steadily, and I picked up the boat without difficulty, raking it through from stern to stem under its protecting canopy. I could see the canopy drop as its supporting metal framework fused in the heat of the ray; flames rose from the interior wooden fittings; the boat's stern seemed to melt away as the thin metal was rendered molten; the water about it boiled under the heat. A cloud of steam then rose up, obscuring it completely from my sight.

I switched off the light. We continued on, rising a little. The steam dissipated. Directly below us on the bubbling, swirling water a few twisted black forms bobbed about. We were so close now I could see them plainly. I looked away hastily.

We swung back toward the Twilight shore, rising sharply. There seemed now only one boat afloat. Far above it I saw a tiny black oblong that I knew was Mercer's platform. A swarm of other dots, with the tiny pencils of red light flashing from them, showed where the cloud of girls were swooping down to the attack. Now that we were out of the action, I had opportunity to watch what was going on more closely.

This last engagement seemed to last less than a minute. The girls darted fearlessly downward among the rays that swung up from the boat. Scores of them were hit; I could see their forms illuminated for an instant by the lurid red and green light. Some passed through it safely; many fell. But those who got within range hit the boat without difficulty. Its lights went out suddenly and a moment later it sank. The girls' lights flashed off, and they rose again into the air—tiny black shapes circling about Mercer's platform.

The scene now seemed suddenly very dark, peaceful and still. A great weight lifted from my heart, though it still remained heavy with what I had seen. I turned to Miela; her face was white and drawn.

"We have won, my girl," I said.

She smiled wanly.

"We have won. But, oh, Alan, that women should have to do such deeds!"

Her eyes shone with the light of a soul in sorrow.

"Pray to your God now, my husband, that this war may be the last, for all time, in all the universe."

THE SIEGE OF THE LONE CITY

Our losses totaled nearly a hundred and fifty girls. We brought back with us on the platforms but six wounded. I shall never forget that hour we spent searching among the wreckage—those blackened, twisted forms of what had once been men and women. I shall not describe it.

Of all the boats which Tao had dispatched on this ill-fated expedition, only one escaped to return with news of the disaster. I was glad now that one, at least, had survived, for the report it would give would, I felt sure, dissuade Tao from making any other similar attempt at invasion.

Our broken little army made its way slowly back to the Great City. We went, not in triumph, but indeed with all the aspect of defeat. The people received us in a frenzy of joy and gratitude to the girls for what they had done.

This first battle took place, as I have said, just after we four had returned from our tour of the Light Country, and before the recruiting of the young men was fairly under way. To this recruiting it proved an extraordinary stimulus. The girls, having been in successful action, stirred the young men of the nation as probably nothing else could, and all over the country they came forward faster than they could be enrolled.

It was two or three days after the battle that Miela came to me one morning with the wounded girl she and I had rescued in the air.

"We have a plan—Sela and I—my husband," she said.

The girl seemed hardly more than a sweet little child—fifteen or sixteen, perhaps. It gave me a shock now to realize that we had allowed her to go into such a combat. One of her blue-feathered wings was bound in a cloth. Its lower portion, I could tell, had been burned away.

"Never will she fly again, my husband," said Miela, "for she is one of those who has sacrificed her wings that we might all be safe from the invader."

She then went on to explain that now, while this feeling of gratitude to the girls ran so high among the people, the time seemed propitious for changing the long-hated law regarding their wings. I had not thought of that, but agreed with her wholly.

I called the people into the castle gardens that same night. Never had I seen such a gathering. We allowed fully ten thousand to come in; the rest we were forced to send away.

157

THE FIRE PEOPLE

Miela made a speech, telling them that in recognition of the girls' services in this war, I had decided to allow them henceforth to keep their wings unmutilated after marriage. We exhibited this little girl, Sela, as one who had given her power of flight, not as a sacrifice on the altar of man's selfishness, but in the service of her country. Then Sela herself made a speech, in her earnest little child voice, pleading for her sisters.

When she ended there may have been some unmarried men in our audience who were still against the measure—doubtless there were—but they were afraid or ashamed to let their feeling be known. When the meeting broke up I had ample evidence of the people's wishes upon which to proceed.

Within a week my congress met, and the law was repealed. We informed the other cities of this action, and everywhere it was met with enthusiasm.

Enlistment and war preparations went steadily on, but despite it all there were more marriages that next month—three times over—than in any before. I had now been in power some three months, and the time was approaching when we were ready to make our invasion of the Twilight Country. We had been maintaining a rigid aërial patrol of the Narrow Sea, but no further activities of the enemy had been threatened.

The expedition, when it was ready, numbered about a thousand young men, each armed with one of the hand light-ray cylinders; fifty officers, and about fifty older men in charge of the projectors and rockets, who, for want of a better term, I might call our artillery corps. There was also the organization of girls, and a miscellaneous corps of men to handle the boats, mechanics to set up the projectors, and a commissariat.

The thousand young men represented those we had selected from the several thousand enlisted in the Great City. All the rest, and the many thousands in the other cities, we were holding in reserve.

We took with us, on this invading expedition, only small-wheeled trucks, on which to convey the larger projectors, and storage tanks and other heavy apparatus, for the Lone City river ran directly to the point where we planned to conduct our siege.

Some forty large boats were required to carry the men, ammunition and supplies. Mercer and I, with Anina and Miela, traveled as before through the air on the two platforms with the girls. We crossed the Narrow Sea without incident and entered the river.

Several hours up, the river narrowed and entered a rocky gorge, four or five hundred feet wide and a thousand feet deep, with almost perpendicular sides. Along one of these ran the Lone City trail. We passed through this gorge. The river here flowed with a current that amounted almost to rapids. Our boats made slow progress. Finally we emerged into an even wilder country, almost devoid of trees. Here we made our first night's encampment.

Noon of the next day found us approaching the Lone City. We did not need to surmise now that Tao would be warned, for far away on the horizon ahead we saw the beams from his great projectors mounting up into the blackness of the sky. Some four miles from the Lone City the river we were ascending swept off to the right. This was its closest point to the city, and here we disembarked. There were several docks and a few houses, but we found them all deserted.

The Lone City was particularly well suited to defense, even though the lay of the country was such that we were enabled to approach here within four miles, and establish our base in comparative safety. The country was wild and rocky, with few trees. The river bed lay in a cañon. From where we landed, a valley so deep and narrow, it might almost be termed a cañon, also led up to the city.

This valley was some two miles wide, with a level floor, and precipitous, rocky sides towering in many places over a thousand feet. Above it stretched a broken plateau country. The valley had many sharp bends and turns, as though in some distant past it had been the bed of a great river that had eroded its tortuous course through the rock.

The Lone City lay shut in at the bottom of this valley between two of its bends. It was a settlement of perhaps ten thousand people, the only city in the Twilight Country, with one exception, on this hemisphere of Mercury.

We established our field base here at the river, and I devoted the next few days to informing myself of the exact lay of the country, and the methods of defense of the city Tao had provided.

I found this defense the height of simplicity, and for its purpose as effective as it well could be. A vertical barrage of light surrounded the city, extending upward into the air with the most powerful projectors some ten or fifteen miles, and, with those of the spreading rays, forming a solid wall of light at the lower altitudes. There were no projectors past the first turn in the valley toward the river—where they could have been directed horizontally—and none of them on the cliff tops above the city.

Thus, although we could not get over this light -barrage, we could approach it closely in many places.

Tao's tactics became immediately evident. He had thrown an almost impregnable barrier close about him and, trusting to its protection, was making no effort to combat us for the moment with any moves of offense.

My first endeavor was to find a position on top of the cliffs from which the city could be reached with a projector. It was practically the only thing to do. The city could not be approached in front from the valley floor; its entire surface beyond the turn was swept by the light -rays. Approach from below in the rear was likewise barred.

Had the barrage been not so high our girls might have flown over it and dropped bombs, or we might have sent rockets over it and dropped them into the city. Neither of these projects was practical. The girls could not fly over that barrage. It was too cold in the higher altitudes. Nor could we send rockets over, for rockets sent through the light were exploded before they could reach their mark.

The projectors along the sides of the city were located for the most part a hundred feet or more back from the base of the surrounding cliffs. This allowed them to cut the cliff face at the top. It will be understood then that we could approach the brink of the cliff in many places, but never sufficiently near to be able to direct our rays downward into the city.

These cliffs were exceedingly jagged and broken. They overhung in many places. Great rifts split them; ravines wound their way down, many of these with small, stunted trees growing in them. A descent from the summit to the floor of the valley, had we been unimpeded by the light, would in many places not have been difficult.

During the next week, we succeeded—working in the prevailing gloom—in establishing a projector at the mouth of a ravine which emerged at the cliff face hardly a hundred feet from the valley bottom. This point was below the spreading light -rays which swept the cliff top above. We mounted the projector without discovery, and, flashing it on suddenly, swept the valley with its rays. An opposing ray from below picked it out almost immediately, and destroyed it, killing two of our men.

The irregularities of the cliffs made several other similar attempts possible. We took advantage of them, and in each case were able to rake the valley with our fire for a moment before our projector was located and destroyed. One, which we were at great pains to protect, was maintained for a somewhat longer period.

I believed we had done an immense amount of damage by these momentarily active projectors, although our enemy gave no sign.

We then tried dropping rockets at the base of the lights in the valley. There were few points at which they could be reached without striking the rays first. But we persisted, sending up a hundred or more. Most were ineffective; a few found their mark, as we could tell by a sudden "hole" in the barrage, which, however, was invariably repaired before we could make it larger.

These activities lasted a week or more. It began, to look as though we had entered upon a lengthy siege. I wondered how long the city's food supply would last if we settled down to starve it out. The thought came to me then that Tao might be almost ready for his second expedition to the earth. Was he indeed merely standing us off in this way so that some day he might depart in his vehicle before our very eyes?

Tao began to adopt our tactics. Without warning one day a projector from a towering eminence near the city flashed down at the river encampment. That we were not entirely destroyed was due to the extreme watchfulness of our guards, who located it immediately with their rays. As it was, we lost nearly a hundred men in the single moment it was in operation.

We then withdrew our camp farther away down the river, to a point where the conformation of the country made a repetition of this attack impossible. A sort of guerrilla warfare now began in the mountains. Our scouting parties frequently met Tao's men, and many encounters, swiftly fatal to one side or the other, took place. But all the time we were able, at intervals, to rake the valley with our fire for brief periods.

Mercer constantly was evolving plans of the utmost daring, most of them indeed amounting practically to suicide for those undertaking them. But I held him back. Our present tactics were dangerous enough, although after the first few fatalities we succeeded in protecting our men, even though our projectors were invariably destroyed.

One of Mercer's plans we tried with some success. There were some places in the light-barrage that were much less high than others. We devised a smaller rocket that could be fired from the platforms. Mercer took it up some twenty thousand feet, and sent several rockets over the light, which we hoped dropped into the city.

A month went by in this way. We were in constant communication by water with the Great City, receiving supplies and reënforcements of men and armament. And then gradually the situation changed. Over a period of several days our hand -to - hand encounters with the enemy grew less frequent. Finally two or three days went by without one of them taking place.

We became bolder and prepared to establish several projectors at different points for simultaneous fire at a given signal. The light -barrage in the valley remained unchanged, although now its beams held steady instead of sometimes swinging to and fro. We dislodged one of its projectors with a rocket, making a hole in the barrage, which this time was not repaired. And then, to our amazement, the lights one by one began to die away. We ceased operations, waiting. Within half a day they had all vanished, like lights which had flickered and burned out.

Mercer, unthinking, was all for an instant attack. We could indeed have swept the valley now without difficulty; but there were thousands of people in the city—non -combatants, women and children—and to murder them to no purpose was not the sort of warfare we cared to make.

It seemed probable that Tao had evacuated his position. The valley beyond the city led up into the mountains toward the Dark City, almost on the borderland of the frozen wastes of the Dark Country. Tao had protected this valley from behind so that we had been unable to penetrate it without making a detour of over twenty miles. This I had not done, although had the siege lasted longer I think with our next reënforcement we should have attempted it.

With the extinguishing of the lights our long -range activities ceased. We anticipated some trick, and for several days remained quiet. Our girls could have flown over the city; but this I would not allow, fearing that a ray would bring them suddenly down.

Miela and myself, occupying one of the stone houses down by the river, held a consultation there with Mercer and Anina.

Mercer, as usual, was for instant action.

"We might as well march right in," he declared. "They're out of business, or they've gone—one or the other."

"To the Dark City they have gone, I think," Anina said.

"I think so, too," Mercer agreed.

"I'll go in alone on foot," I said, "and find out what has happened."

But Miela shook her head.

"One who can fly will go more safely. I shall go."

"Not you, my sister," Anina said quietly. "Warfare is not for you—now. That you can understand, can you not? I shall go."

Mercer insisted on accompanying her; and he did, part of the way, waiting while she flew close over the city. It was several hours before they returned, reporting that the place was almost in ruins, and that Tao and his men had fled some time before, leaving the light-barrage to burn itself out. The next day, with our men in the black cloth suits of armor marching up the valley, and the girls with their black shields flying overhead, we took possession of all that remained of the Lone City.

THE END OF TAO

The scene of desolation that met us in the Lone City was at once extraordinary and awesome. It seemed impossible that our rays, acting for so brief a period, could have done so much damage. The city was nothing more than a semicivilized settlement of little, flat -topped stone houses. Our rays, striking these, had discharged harmlessly into the ground. But the interiors had been penetrated through windows and doors, and everything inflammable about them, as well as about the streets, had been destroyed.

The people had taken refuge in cellars underground and in caves and crevices—wherever they could find shelter. But even so, there were a thousand dead in that city that morning, and rapidly spreading disease would shortly have killed them all. They came out of their hiding places little by little as we entered the streets, and stood about in groups staring at us sullenly. They seemed mostly old men and women and children, the younger men having fled with Tao's army. They were heavy -set, pathetic people, with broad, heavy faces, pasty -white skin, and large protruding eyes. We were in the Lone City nearly a month, burying the dead, doing what we could for the people, and destroying or removing the apparatus Tao had left behind him.

The Lone City, before the banishment of Tao, had been one of the most primitive settlements of the Twilight region. It was in the other hemisphere that the Twilight Country was more densely populated; but since this Lone City was so close to the Great City it had become the scene of Tao's exile.

This region about the Lone City was of the most barren of the whole Twilight country. Its people were almost entirely meat eaters. Back toward the Dark Country great bands of animals like caribou roamed. Living almost entirely in darkness, they had little power of sight, and were easy prey to hunters.

Their hides, which were covered with short, white fur, provided clothing; a form of candle was made from their fat, and used for lighting; and their flesh provided food. The Dark City, some two hundred and fifty miles away, was the center from which most of these animals were obtained.

"Then, that's where Tao has been getting his supplies from," Mercer exclaimed, as we heard all this from one of the Twilight People. "And that's where he has gone now."

Tao had indeed withdrawn to the Dark City, we learned positively. And more than that, we learned that he had factories there as well as here. We found in the Lone City some eight of the interplanetary vehicles—most of them almost entirely completed. The fact that Tao had abandoned them so readily made us believe he had others in the Dark City.

There seemed a curious lack of appliances for protection against the ray. This we attributed to two causes—that Tao had managed to take most of them with him, and that his supply of fabric came from distant cities on the other side of the globe. Within a month after we had occupied the Lone City we were again ready to start forward. It had been an irksome month for Mercer, and not a day had passed without my receiving a truculent declaration from him that we were fools to allow Tao to escape so easily.

Our occupation of the Lone City was to continue. On this second expedition farther into the Twilight Country I took with me a much smaller and more select force. We had before us a land journey of some two hundred and fifty miles, through an unknown, barren country, in which it would be difficult for us to maintain ourselves, so I was determined to be burdened with as few men as possible.

Our force consisted of all the older men trained in the operation of the larger projectors and rockets; a variety of mechanics and helpers, men selected for their physical strength; a corps of young men to the number of fifty, and fifty girls.

We did not take the platforms, for I assumed it would be too cold for the girls to make sustained flights. Against this cold we provided ourselves well with the white furry garments of the Twilight People. I need not go into details of our march to the Dark City. It occupied some three weeks. We met with no opposition, passing a few isolated settlements, whose inhabitants rather welcomed us than otherwise.

This region we passed through took us almost to the ill-defined borders of the Dark Country. It was not mountainous, but rather more a great broken plateau with a steady ascent. Each day it grew darker and colder, until at last we entered perpetual night. It was not the sort of night we know on earth, but a Stygian blackness.

We used little torches now, of the light-ray current, and our little army, trudging along in their lurid glare, and dragging its wagons piled high with the projectors, presented a curious and weird picture. The country for the most part was barren rock, with a few stunted trees growing in the ravines and crevices. There was an abundance of water.

We encountered several rainstorms, and once during the last week it snowed a little. Except for the storms, the wind held steady, a gentle breeze from the colder regions in front blowing back toward the Light Country behind us.

During the latter days of our journey I noticed a curious change in the ground. It seemed now, in many places, to be like a soft, chalky limestone, which ran in pockets and seams between strata of very hard rock. I called Miela's attention to it once, and she pointed out a number of irregular shaped, small masses of a substance which in daylight I assumed might be yellow. These were embedded in the soft limestone.

"Sulphur," she said. "Like that on your earth. There is much of it up here, I have heard."

The Dark City occupied a flat plateau, slightly elevated above the surrounding country, and on the brink of a sheer drop of some six or seven thousand feet to an arm of the polar sea.

Our problems now were very different from when we had laid siege to the Lone City. The conformation of the country allowed us no opportunity to approach closer than two or three miles to the barrage of light we must expect. We could not reach the city from these nearest points with our projectors.

There were many lateral ravines depressed below the upper surface of the main plateau, and though the light-rays from the city, directed horizontally, would sweep their tops, we found we could traverse many of them a considerable distance in safety. But from the bottoms of them we could only fire our rockets without specific aim and our projectors not at all.

Only by the most fortuitous of circumstances did we escape complete annihilation the first moment we appeared within range. We had no idea what lay ahead—although the guides we had brought with us from the Lone City informed us we were nearing our destination—and the scene remained in complete darkness until we were hardly more than five miles outside Tao's stronghold.

Then, without warning, his lights flashed on—not only a vertical barrage, but a horizontal one as well—sweeping the higher points of the entire country around for a distance of twelve or fifteen miles.

We were, at the moment, following the bottom of a narrow gully. Had we been on any of the upper reaches of the plateau we would undoubtedly have been picked out by one of the roving beams of light and destroyed.

We camped where we were, and again for several days I attempted nothing, devoting myself to a thorough exploration of the country about us. The Dark City appeared impregnable. Beams of light from Tao's larger projectors were constantly roaming about the entire plateau that surrounded it, and every higher point of vantage from which one of ours could have reached them must have been struck by their rays a score of times a day.

It will be understood, of course, that any place where we could mount one of the higher powered projectors, a task of several hours at best, and strike the city, must of necessity be also within range of their rays, for theirs were as powerful as ours. Upon observation I felt convinced that should we attempt to mount a projector anywhere on these higher points it would be sought out and destroyed long before we could bring it into action.

That this was Tao's stronghold, and not the Lone City, now became evident. I could readily understand why he had retreated here. Fully four times as many projectors as he had in operation in the Lone City were now in evidence. Those of shorter range, and spreading rays, kept the entire country bathed in steady light for several miles around him, while the larger ones—a hundred of them possibly—roved constantly over the black emptiness beyond.

From our encampment we could advance but little farther. Fortunately, retreat was open to us; and once beyond the circle of steady light, we had no difficulty in moving about in the darkness, even though momentarily we frequently were within range of the single light -beams, had they chanced to swing upon us.

This was the situation which, even Mercer agreed, appeared hopeless. We explored the brink of the precipice below which lay the sea. It was a sheer drop of many thousand feet. Although a descent might have been made closer to the Dark City, certainly it was not possible at any point we could reach. We sent our girls down, and they reported that from below it appeared probable that access to the ocean was had by the Dark City some miles farther along. They went but a short distance, for Tao's lights were occasionally sweeping about; and more than that, they could make but very short flights, owing to the cold.

To starve Tao out appeared equally as impractical as a direct attack. With our little army we could not surround the city on a circumference of some eighty miles.

THE FIRE PEOPLE

We might, indeed, have barred the several roads that entered it, but it seemed probable that if Tao wanted to come out he would come, for all we could do to stop him. And yet to starve him out seemed our only possible plan.

"We'll have to send back for reënforcements," I told Mercer, Miela and Anina at one of our many conferences. "An army of several thousand, if we can maintain it up here."

And then, the very next day, Mercer and Anina came forward with their discovery. We had set up our encampment of little black fabric tents in a ravine some six miles outside the city, securely hidden by surrounding cliffs. Above us across the black sky the greenish-red beams of Tao's light-rays swept continually to and fro. Miela and I were sitting together disconsolately in our tent, reviewing the situation, when Mercer and Anina burst in. They had been roaming about together, exploring the country, and came in now full of excitement and enthusiasm to tell us what they had found. We two were to accompany them. They would tell us no more than that; and as soon as we had all eaten we started off. It would be a trip of several hours, Mercer said, and would take us around to the other side and partly behind the Dark City.

We followed no road, but scrambled along over the open country, picking our way as best we could, and using the lights from the city to give us direction. The two girls half walked, half flew, and Mercer and I, with our ability to take huge leaps, made rapid progress.

The night was black—that unluminous blackness that seems to swallow everything, even objects near at hand. We made our way along, using little hand search-lights that threw a red glare a short distance before us.

We kept down in the gulleys as much as possible, avoiding the higher places where Tao's long-range beams were constantly striking, and passed around in front of the Dark City, keeping always at least five miles away.

We had been traveling two or three hours, and still Mercer and Anina gave us no clew to what we were about to see. It began to snow. Huge, soft flakes soon lay thick on the ground.

"Mercer, where are you taking us?" I exclaimed once.

"You shall see very soon now," Anina answered me. "What we have found, Ollie and I—and our plan—you shall understand it soon."

We had to be content with that. An hour later we found ourselves well around behind the Dark City and hardly more than four miles outside it. A great jagged cliff -face, two hundred feet high perhaps, fronted us. We, at its base, were on comparatively low ground here, with another low line of cliffs shading us from the light -beams of the city.

Mercer and Anina stopped and pointed upward at the cliff. A huge seam of the soft, chalky limestone ran laterally for five hundred feet or more across its face. I saw embedded in this seam great irregular masses of sulphur.

"There you are," said Mercer triumphantly. "Sulphur—stacks of it. All we have to do is set fire to it. With the wind blowing this way—right toward the city—" His gesture was significant.

The feasibility of the plan struck us at once. It was an enormous deposit of free sulphur. From this point the prevailing wind blew directly across the city. The sulphur lay in great masses sufficiently close together so that if we were to set fire to it in several places with our small light -ray torches we could be assured of its burning steadily. And its fumes, without warning, blowing directly over the city—I shuddered as the whole thing became clear to me.

"Good God, man—"

"That'll smoke 'em out," declared Mercer, waving his hand again toward the cliff. "I ask you now, won't that smoke 'em out?"

"Tao's men—yes." Miela's face was grave as she answered Mercer's triumphant question. "It will do that, Ollie. Kill them all, of a certainty; but that whole city there—"

Mercer stared at his feet, toying idly with the little torch in his hand.

"Can you think of any other way to get at Tao?" he asked.

Anina met my eyes steadily.

"There is no other way," she said quietly. "It must be done. It is your world—your people—we must think of now. And you know there is no other way."

We decided at last to try it. Once we had made the decision, we proceeded as quickly as possible to put the plan into execution. We moved our encampment farther away, well out of danger from the fumes.

We mounted several of the projectors in positions where their rays could reach the surrounding country, and the sky, although not the city itself. Then, ordering our men and girls to hold themselves in readiness for whatever might occur, we four went off together to fire the sulphur.

THE FIRE PEOPLE

The wind was blowing directly toward the city as we stood at the base of the cliff, a silent little group. I think that now, at this moment, we all of us hesitated in awe at what we were about to do.

Mercer broke the tension.

"Come on, Alan—let's start it off. Now is the time—a lot of places at once."

We flashed on our little light-rays, and in a moment the sulphur was on fire at a score of different points. We drew off a few hundred feet to one side and sat down to watch it in the darkness. Overhead Tao's red beams swept like giant search-lights across the inky sky.

The sulphur started burning with tiny little spots of wavering blue flame that seemed, many of them, about to die away. Gradually they grew larger, spreading out slowly and silently in ever-widening circles. Under the heat of the flames the sulphur masses became molten, turned into a viscous dark red fluid that boiled and bubbled heavily and dropped spluttering upon the ground.

Slowly the blue-green flames spread about, joining each other and making more rapid headway—a dozen tiny volcanoes vomiting their deadly fumes and pouring forth their sluggish, boiling lava. The scene about us now was lighted in a horrible blue-green glare. A great cloud of thin smoke gathered, hung poised a moment, and then rolled slowly away—its deadly fumes hanging low to the ground and spreading ever wider as though eager to clutch the unsuspecting city in their deadly embrace.

The entire face of the cliff was now covered with the crawling blue fire, lapping avidly about with its ten-foot tongues. We drew back, staring silently at each other's ghastly green faces.

"Let's—let's get away," Mercer whispered finally. "No use staying here now."

We hurried back to the nearest place where one of our projectors was set up. The two men guarding it looked at us anxiously, and smiled triumphantly when Miela told them what we had done. We stood beside them a moment, then Miela and I climbed to an eminence near by from which we had an unobstructed view of the city.

The light-barrage still held steady. The individual, higher-powered projectors as before swung their beams lazily about the country. We sat partly in the shelter of a huge bowlder, behind which we could have dropped quickly had one of them turned our way.

"Soon it will be there," Miela said softly, when we had been sitting quiet for a time.

I did not answer. It was indeed too solemn a thing for words, this watching from the darkness while an invisible death, let loose by our own hands, stole down upon our complacent enemies.

A few moments more we watched—and still the scene before us showed no change. Then, abruptly, the lights seemed to waver; some of the beams swung hurriedly to and fro, then remained motionless in unusual positions, as though the men at their levers in sudden panic had abandoned them.

My heart was beating violently. What hidden tragedy was being enacted behind that silent barrier of light? I shuddered as my imagination conjured up hideous pictures of that unseen death that now must be stalking about those city streets, entering those homes, polluting the air with its stifling, noisome breath, and that even at this distance seemed clutching at my own lungs.

I suppose the whole thing did last only a moment. There was little in what we saw of significance had we not known. But we did know—and the knowledge left us trembling and unnerved.

I leaped to my feet, pulling Miela after me, and in a few moments more we were back beside the projector we had left with Mercer and Anina. Suddenly a white shape appeared in the sky over the city. It passed perilously close above the shattered light -barrage and came sailing out in our direction.

Mercer jumped for the projector, but I was nearer, and in a moment I had flashed it on.

"It's Tao!" Mercer shouted. "He—"

It was one of Tao's interplanetary vehicles, rising slowly in a great arc above us. I swung our light -beams upward; it swept across the sky and fell upon the white shape; the thing seemed to poise in its flight, as though held by the little red circle of light that fastened upon it, boring its way in. Then, slowly at first, it fell; faster and faster it dropped, until it struck the ground with a great crash—the first and only sound of all this soundless warfare.

It was three days before the great sulphur deposit we had ignited burned itself out. The lights of the city had all died away, and blackness such as I never hope to experience again settled down upon the scene.

We approached the Dark City then; we even entered one or two of its outlying houses;, but beyond that we did not go, for we had made certain of what we wanted to know.

THE FIRE PEOPLE

I remember my father once describing how, when a young man, he had gone to the little island of Martinique shortly after the great volcanic outbreak of Mount Pelée. I remember his reluctance to dwell upon the scenes he saw there in that silent city of St. Pierre—the houses with their dead occupants, stricken as they were sitting about the family table; the motionless forms in the streets, lying huddled where death had overtaken them in their sudden panic. That same reluctance silences me now, for one does not voluntarily dwell upon such scenes as those.

A day or so later we found the interplanetary projectile which had sought to escape. Amid its wreckage lay the single, broken form of Tao—that leader who, plotting the devastation of two worlds for his own personal gain, had at the very last deserted his comrades and met his death alone.

THE RETURN

There is but little more to add. With the death of Tao and the changing of the law concerning the virgins' wings, my mission on Mercury was over. But I did not think of that then, for with the war ended, my position as virtual ruler of the Light Country still held Mercer and me occupied with a multiplicity of details. It was a month or more after our return from the Twilight Country that Miela reminded me of father and my duty to him. "You have forgotten, my husband. But I have not. Your world—it calls you now. You must go back."

Go back home—to father and dear little Beth! I had not realized how much I had wanted it.

"What you have done for our nation—for our girls—can never be repaid, Alan. And you can do more in later years, perhaps. But now your father needs you—and we must think of him."

I cast aside every consideration of what changes would first have to be made here on Mercury, and decided in that moment to go.

"But you must go with me, Miela," I said, and then, as I thought of something else, I added gently: "You will, won't you, little wife? For you know I cannot leave you now."

She smiled her tender little smile.

"'Whither thou goest, I will go,' my husband," she quoted softly, "'for thy people shall be my people, and thy God my God.'"

We were ready to start at the time of the next inferior conjunction of Mercury with the earth. At our combined pleading, and with the permission of his associates, Fuero was persuaded to take command of the nation during my absence; and I felt I was leaving affairs in able hands.

Lua refused to accompany us; but she urged Anina to go, and the little girl was ready enough to take advantage of her mother's permission.

Though he said nothing, I shall never forget Mercer's face as this decision was made.

The vehicle in which Miela had made her former trip was still lying in the valley where we had left it. We went away privately, only Lua and Fuero accompanying us out of the city.

Lua parted with her two daughters quietly. Her emotions at seeing them go she concealed under that sweet, gentle reserve which was characteristic of her always.

THE FIRE PEOPLE

"Promise me you will be careful of her, Alan," she said softly as she kissed me at parting.

We landed in the Chilean Andes, with that patient statue of the Christ to welcome us back to earth. The Trans -Andean Railroad runs near it, and we soon were in the city of Buenos Aires. The two girls, with wings shrouded in their long cloaks, walked about its crowded streets with a wonderment I can only vaguely imagine. We had only what little money I had taken with me to Mercury. I interviewed a prominent banker of the city, told him in confidence who I was, and from him obtained necessary funds.

We cabled father then, and he answered at once that he would come down and join us. We waited for him down there, and in another month he was with us—dear old gentleman, leaning over the steamer rail, trying to hold back the tears of joy that sprang into his eyes at sight of me. Little Beth was with him, too, smart and stylish as ever, and good old Bob Trevor, whom she shyly presented as her husband.

The beach at Mar del Plata, near Buenos Aires, is one of the most beautiful spots in South America; and on a clear moonlit night, with the Southern Cross overhead, it displays the starry heavens as few other places can on this earth.

On such a night in February, 1942, Mercer and Anina sat together on the sand, apart from the gay throng that crowded the pavilion below them. The girl was dressed all in white, with a long black cape covering her wings. Her beautiful blond hair was piled on her head in huge soft coils, and over it she had thrown a filmy, sky -blue mantilla that shone with a soft luster in the moonlight and seemed reflected in the blue of her eyes.

Mercer in white flannels sat beside her, cross -legged on the white sand, with a newly purchased Hawaiian guitar across his lap. From the band stand in the pavilion down the beach faint strains of music floated up to them. The moon silvered the water before them; a soft, gentle breeze of summer caressed their cheeks; the myriad stars glittered overhead like brilliant gems scattered on the turquoise velvet of the sky.

Anina, chin cupped in her hand, sat staring at the wonderful heavens that all her life before had been withheld from her sight. She sighed tremulously.

"I want to say this is a night," Mercer declared, breaking a long silence.

"It's—it's beautiful," she answered softly. "Those millions of worlds—like mine, perhaps—or like this one of yours." She turned to him. "Ollie, which of them is my world?"

174

"You can't see it now, Anina. It's too close to the sun."

Again she sighed. "I'm sorry for that. It would seem closer, perhaps, if we could see it."

"You're not sorry you came, Anina? You don't want to go back now?"

"Not now, Ollie." She smiled into his earnest, pleading eyes. "For those I love are here as well as there. I have Miela and Alan—and—"

"And?" Mercer leaned forward eagerly.

"And Miela's little son—that darling little baby. We must go back soon and see Miela. She will be wondering where we are."

Mercer sat back. "Oh," he said. "Yes, we must."

The band in the pavilion stopped its music. Mercer slid his little steel cross-piece over the guitar strings and began to play the haunting, crying music of the islands, the music of moonlight and love. After a moment he stopped abruptly.

"Anina, that little song you sang in the boat that day—you remember—the day we went to the Water City? Sing it again, Anina."

She sang it through softly, just as she had in the boat, to its last ending little half-sob.

Mercer laid his guitar on the sand beside him.

"You said that music talks to you, Anina—though sometimes you—you don't understand just what it tries to say. I feel it that way, too—only—only to-night—now—I think I do understand."

His voice was very soft and earnest and just a trifle husky.

"You said that it was a love-song, Anina, and it was sad because love is sad. Do you—think love is always sad?" He put out his hand awkwardly and touched hers.

"Do you, Anina?" he whispered.

Her little figure swayed toward him. She half turned, and in her shining eyes he saw the light that needs no words to make its meaning clear.

The timidity that so often before had restrained him was swept away; he took her abruptly into his arms, kissing her hair, her eyes, her lips.

"Love isn't—always very sad, is it, Anina?"

Her arms held him close.

"I—I don't know," she breathed against his shoulder. "But it's—it's very—wonderful."

www.ingramcontent.com/pod-product-compliance
Lightning Source LLC
Chambersburg PA
CBHW051823170626
46807CB00003B/1008